GONE 2 €UROPE...

...£EAVE A ME$$AGE

WRITTEN
BY

BRANDON
SINCLAIR

Goldstein Publishing Group

Gone to Europe, Leave a Message

All characters appearing in this work are fictitious. Any resemblance to real persons, living or dead is purely coincidental. The wording of this disclaimer differs from jurisdiction, and from country to country, as does its legal effectiveness.

Copyright© 2011 by Goldstein Publishing Group, llc

All rights reserved. No part of this book may be reproduced or transmitted in any form or by any means without written permission from the author.

ISBN (978-0-615-48495-2)

Acknowledgments

First, I would like to thank God, in which all things are made possible. Next, I have to thank my mom and dad for their unwavering love and respect.

I would also like to thank my grandparents, Jessie and Bernadine, for their love and guidance, of which I will always be grateful for. Additionally, I would like to acknowledge my publishers for taking a chance on me as well as for their patience. I am so very appreciative.

Furthermore, I owe a great deal of gratitude to Dean Fox, Brahn Jenkins, Meagan Sweeny, and Noelle Harper for their expertise and technical assistance. And certainly a very special shout out goes to the Howell family for their constant love and support.

Last but surely not least, I must acknowledge my alma mater, North Carolina Agriculture and Technical State University for the invaluable life lessons it taught me in which I could not function without. (AGGIE PRIDE!!!)

This book is dedicated to Linda McKinnon, Norman "Billy Red" Whitaker, and Aaron "And1" Smiley.

"Weeping may endure for a night, but joy cometh early in the morning." —Pslam 30:5

Chapter 1

"Mel!...Hey Mel! Wake up!
"Huh?"
"Dude, Wake Up!"
"I'm up, man!"
"Did you feed the dogs yet?"
Like really, how could I have fed the dogs if I'm just waking up? I never feed the dogs and go back to sleep. To be in his trimester of med school, my brother asks the dumbest questions. He was just getting off of his second job at the soda plant.

"You need to hurry up and get dressed if you want a ride to the subway" he said before walking back to his room.

"What time is it?" I asked.
I looked at my half-broken alarm clock and saw it was almost 7:30. I had to be at work in an hour and my train took at least 35 minutes to get there. I hopped up and took a

three minute shower, totally skipped ironing my clothes and grabbed my laptop. As I walked in to the living room I could hear the dogs whining. I put my laptop down and went to get their food out of the laundry room.

One cupful each for badass #1 and badass #2! Of course that wasn't their real names, but there was no greater description. All they ever did was eat and tear shit up. I mean what the hell is a Labradoodle anyway? Some sap out there thought it'd be cute to mate their Labrador Retriever with a Poodle, only to create the most annoying dog on Earth. Why would I speak so harsh about my dogs? That's just it, they weren't my dogs. Although one would assume so seeing that I was the only one that looked after them. They were my brother's fiancés' dogs. My brother spoils that chick rotten. She's probably the reason why he works so many damn jobs. He got them for her because she just "haddd to have them". Her apartment doesn't allow her to have any pets so Jeff, my brother, being the shmuck that he is, told her it would be okay for them to stay here.

He was only two years older than me; people that know us say that I was born with the looks and he was given the brains. I suppose I got the short end of that stick. I mean who needs looks when you're about to be an M.D.

Jeff met his fiancé at a Sorority probate two years ago. I have no idea what she does for a living but I do know that she was hardly ever here to take care of these damn puppies, and neither was he. There'd been plenty of afternoons in which I came home to an apartment heavily scented with piss. Fortunately for me, I was moving out at the end of the month so that the love birds can have a hearth of their own before jumping the broom.

Badass 1 and 2 both scarped down all of their food without looking up or even taking a breath. The girl dog (Badass #1) came over to me and looked me up and down and started to bark.

"I don't have time for this. I'm going to be late for work" I said hovering over her.

Her small puppy bark turned into whining, which triggered the boy dog's (Badass #2) whining; which absolutely drove me nuts! I grabbed my jacket, "fine let's go and make it quick."

I led them outside, and to my surprise the neighborhood kids were just now getting on to the school bus. I suppose everyone was running a little behind this morning. After several minutes of sniffing trees and licking dirt they finally used it. I hurried them back inside and directed them to their crates. The boy dog trotted in to his crate to play with his bone. The girl dog then sat down in front of me and stared again.

"What is it now?"

She leaped up and bit me on the hand with her sharp puppy teeth, then walked back to her crate as to say next time don't take so long. Damn she's rude. One of these days I was going to call the humane society on my brother, but for now I needed a ride to the station. I ran in to his room to find him sleeping on the floor with his shoes still on.

"Hey Jeff, Wake Up! Let me get a ride to the train station.

He turned over and in his sleepy tone said "did you feed the dogs?"

"Yes mannn, now let me get a ride. I can't be late."

I arrived to the station noticing everyone running to catch the 8:00 train. As I walked towards the door the old man passing out newspapers told me to hurry because the train was leaving in two minutes. I ran down the escalator but just remembered that I needed to add more money to my smart trip card. I ran up to the machine, scanned my card and entered a five. I then said excuse me as I ran pass an old lady carrying a big bright yellow shoulder bag. I scanned my card to pass the turn tolls and ran up the steps to get to the train. The doors were closing as soon as I got to the train. I stuck one arm in the train car just as the doors closed. To my surprise they shut and clasped on to my arm—which they're not supposed to do. I quickly pried my arm out and stood back from the rail. Luckily the doors opened back up allowing me to enter.

  At a seat near the back of the train car, I sat and took a deep breath. All I could do was pray that the day got better. As I looked down I saw a big bright yellow shoulder bag next to a woman. It was the same old woman that I ran pass just a minute ago. She was sitting back in her chair sleeping. How peculiar. Looking at her bag reminded me that I forgot my own laptop bag. Frustrated, I thought to myself if it wasn't for Badass 1 and 2, I wouldn't have to go through this shit every day. Ten feet beyond the platform out into the tunnel and the trained stalled.

"Oh Lord, please get this train moving" said an old man sitting behind me—which is exactly what I was thinking. After about five minutes it began to move again. The NYC transit system can be so unreliable at times.

I put my head phones on and cranked up my iPod. I closed my eyes but not all the way. This was in fear of falling asleep and missing my stop like I did last week.

Chapter 2

The train was ahead of schedule that day. It only took twenty five minutes to get to the city. I hurried up the street towards my job; I had nine minutes to walk four blocks.

"Awesome, plenty of time to make it," I assured myself.

I walked so fast that there was double the cold smoke from the breaths I took. Finally, I got to my building and upon entering the doors one of the security guards stopped me. It was Mrs. Rosa, an eccentric but nice, older dame that always spoke to everyone that entered the building.

"Son, you're about to be late! Ooh and you're breathing so hard. Have you been running in that cold air out there? You gon' get walking pneumonia."

"Yes…I'm running late" I responded trying to walk around her.

"Hey look… I've been listening to that cd you made me and I love it…It's so soulful." Her speech seemed to accelerate by the second. I didn't want to be rude to her because she was probably the nicest person in the entire building, but I had to do something in order to make it in on time.

I smiled and quickly responded "I'm glad you like it. I like it too; as a matter of fact I'm going make you another one right now, I gotta run. See ya later. Have a good day."

I caught the elevator doors opening just as I approached. When I got in I glanced at my watch and saw that I had a minute left. Damn this elevator! It was stopping on every floor on the way up to mine. Finally, the doors opened and I gave a quick hello nod to the receptionist as I walked straight to my desk. I looked over and luckily my supervisor wasn't there yet. Thank God. I sat down and caught my breath as I logged into my computer.

"MEL! IS THAT BATCH READY YET?!!" Ms. Schmidt screamed from across the aisle. "I have to post some stuff before noon. I need all of those docs on your desk taken care of before lunch! Can you do that?!"

"Sure thing Ms. Schmidt", I responded.

"Oh, and these too."
She strolled over to my desk and dropped a huge stack of papers on top of it, causing the previous pile to now resemble a jenga tower. I was no stranger to hard work but this was just plain ridiculous. How the hell was I supposed to get this done before noon?

"I have a meeting with Peterson so mind the phone calls too" she added.

Staring at the towering stack of documents that stood before me, I refused to let the fact that my four foot cubicle was starting to make me claustrophobic hinder me. I refused to let the fact that my computer ran slower than a 1988 Apple computer, deter me. I refused to let the fact that my boss's cubicle was right behind mine, pressure me. I had to get it done, and I was going to get it done…before noon!

    I reached in to my desk drawer and pulled out a stick of gum, although I would have preferred cigarette instead. One by one I took every document from the pile and processed them. When my desk phone rang, I sent the calls to voicemail. All morning I worked without so much as inching away from my desk; not even to take a bathroom break.

Halfway through the pile my fingers began to cramp from rigorous typing. I worked through the pain. Finally, I was down to the last few. I made sure to save the batch just as a precaution. Not too soon after that, with three docs to go, the system locked me out—total shutdown. I looked about the room and everyone else's computer was working fine.

"She's coming back" I heard my co-worker Sharon whisper from across the room. At that point the only thing I could do was send the reports without including the three remaining documents. Of course I'd catch hell about it later.

Ms. Schmidt walked in with a look of frustration on her face. Peterson, her boss, was an asshole but in a polite kind of way. (Kind of like the boss in that one movie, *Office Space*) He must have chewed her out and now, here she came to take it out on everybody else.

"Mel! Why didn't you answer your phone I've been calling you. Where's that batch? Did you finish it?!"

"Yes Ms. Schmidt I exported it to the database, I answered.

I looked over to see Sharon and Ellen giggling at their desks. Fourteen data entry clerks in our department, and she rarely gave anyone else a hard time. Perhaps being the only black person on our team granted me that privilege. If it weren't for the temp, Saleem from Mumbai, I would swear she had some sort of grudge against minorities.

Ms. Schmidt was the most fucked up boss anyone could have. Egotistical, verbally abusive, and childish, she was the typical adult bully. I'm no psychologist but it was well apparent that she suffered from repressed feelings of being teased for being overweight much of her life. She had gotten lap band surgery and a breast reduction around this time last year. It was a good thing she was starting to gain some of her weight back; with a head of that capacity, her body was disproportioned to the point where she resembled a realistic bobble head doll. Her voice was irritating to say the least, and her hygiene was morbid. She smelled as if she'd gone for a swim in the East River along with the application of cheap perfume. Secretly, everyone called her Ms. Shit behind her back because her breath was the equivalent of a city landfill, or better yet New Jersey's drinking water.

It was twelve o'clock, aka break time. I went to get a drink of water and to the restroom. My hands ached something terrible from typing. I went to wash them and found myself gazing in to the mirror with the three remaining docs on my mind……

Returning to my desk all I could hear was someone shouting my name.

There was absolutely no surprise as to whom it was.

"Mel! Where have you been?"

"I went to the restroom."

"There are three docs missing from this report and THOSE ARE THE THREE I NEED TO SUBMIT TO CORPORATE FOR REVIEW, she screamed."

I thought to myself, *then why the hell did she put them at the bottom of the stack.*

"I got locked out of the system as I was putting them in" I responded.

"Don't give me excuses. I need those entered right now!"

"Yes Ma'am."

I took my seat and tried my best to log back in, but nothing was working. I could hear her on the phone shouting at someone from IT. Her voice was starting to annoy me so I put my headphones on and turned up the volume to block it out. Finally, the system let me back in. I entered the last three docs and began resending the report. Before I could finish she tapped me on my shoulder and pulled my earphone out.

"Hey dummy…I've been calling you for the past five minutes! I need you to enter these docs that just came through the fax!"
She dropped a stack of damn near a hundred papers on my desk and walked back to her desk talking shit. I stared at this stack for about 30 seconds, which simultaneously was the time it took my blood to reach a temperature twice that of boiling point. All thoughts of a promotion in the near future escaped my mind. *I know this fat bitch didn't just call me a dummy!*
My blood temperature began to rise 3 times beyond boiling point, in fact, to the point where I was about to hulk out of my shirt. Enough was enough. I pushed away from my desk so hard that my chair hit the back part of my cubicle knocking the plant from her shelf over on to her desk. I grabbed the stack of documents as I got up and turned to face her and her "delayed" reaction of shock.

"TO HELL WITH THESE FUCKING DOCUMENTS…YOU DO IT!!!" I shouted. I held the stack square in both hands and punted them across the hall as if I was field goal kicker, Jason Elam.

"If you say one more word to me, I swear I'm going to staple your fucking mouth shut!"

I grabbed my jacket and my work keys off of my desk and knocked the papers off her desk as I passed. [Yea, it was a little immature but it was the next best thing to punching someone.] I headed straight to Peterson's office. I could see that he was on the telephone so I quietly entered and slammed dunked his 5 foot toy basketball goal, managing to purposely bend the rim. He looked up at me in bewilderment as I smiled while giving him the finger, and quietly exiting. I made sure to close the door behind me. Suddenly, I was tackled by the other security guards, and then tossed out of the building like Jazzy Jeff from Fresh Prince of Bel-Air…..

Interrupted by a flush from the next stall, I awoke from my temporary delusional state of liberation. I rarely had the time to day dream but when I did this one was always my favorite, minus the getting tackled and thrown out by security part. For some odd reason I could never make a smooth exit in that dream.

When I returned to my desk (for real this time) I held my head in sorrow and began to think about what was keeping me at this Hell hole. This place didn't suit me at all. It was as if I were a slave that had been set free and decided to stay, out of some unknown fear. But then again, there was also the fear of letting my mother down. Remembering her face when I got the job, she was so relieved of not having to share the burden of helping me pay back my student loan.

As strong willed as I thought myself to be, I couldn't quit. After all, there were some pros. Over three years of work experience, okay health insurance, and not to mention I had saved over ten percent of the purchase price for a down payment on a condo in Brooklyn.

Although, how I wound up in a data entry job is still a wonder to me. Four years prior, I'd graduated from Penn State with a dual degree in English and World History.

Currently, I chose to blame it on the effects of a screwed up economy rather than lack of ambition on my part.

Although I couldn't call my job a desirable career, I'd have to be a fool to quit now. I considered the advice my brother gave me a week ago: "Sometimes you have to make the sacrifice now in order to be where you want to be later in life".

But with all of this stress would there even be a later? And would it really be worth it? Since working here I had developed a smoking addiction, bladder complications, and let's not forget about the shingles I contracted from stress following last year's close. What was next, a stomach ulcer? Or even worse, going bald? I hated this place. At the moment I would rather take Spike Lee's advice from the early 80's and burn it down.

In the middle of my self-pity, I could hear Ms. Schmidt tromping down the hallway rattling the cubicles as she walked.

"MEL!!! This batch is incomplete! Do you not have the sense to complete 'the' simplest task!?"

"Ms. Schmidt I tried to complete it but the system crashed."

"Well the minute…No the second, that it's back up and running I want this report completed!" she said crotched over and shouting at the side of my face.

"I'm going to lunch and there'd better be a completed report on my desk when I get back."

"Yes Ms. Shit…I mean Ms. Schmidt."
She gave me a stern look and then walked away.

This should qualify as harassment. Her breath smelled like soiled baby diapers. No one should have to endure that kind of persecution. I could only imagine that this and her foul attitude were the biggest contributors to her not having a man; or a woman in any case.

Sharon and Ellen giggled from across the room. They often stated how much they hated this job, but seeing how amused they were I really couldn't tell.
I needed a cigarette…like now.

I took the stairs up to the outside terrace for a quick smoke. Perhaps the cold air would do me some good. My usual melodramatic day dream of me quitting was constantly interrupted with visions of the ridicule that had just taken place. Maybe one day the Lord will give me the courage to quit or perhaps a sign that it's time to move on.

I wrapped up my smoke break and headed back feeling a little better than before. Suddenly, I felt a wave of depression sweep over me the closer I approached my desk. I then took a few steps back and the depression started to disappear. Slowly I walked forward again, and again I felt the presence of sadness. Finally, a voice in my head said "*keep going*".
Assuming that this was my conscious, I decided to listen to it and continued to walk. I noticed an instant change in my mood. I proceeded to the elevators; continued from the elevators to the bottom floor, and then towards the exit.

I saw Mrs. Rosa ahead holding her walkie talkie as I was leaving.
Just then. "OH FUCK!"...*Not now. Really?*
Ms. Schmidt had just walked through the revolving door holding a bucket of chicken in one hand and her hand bag in the other.

"That batch report better be complete" she chimed across the lobby in a polite but obnoxious tone.

"Um…yes they are" I hesitated. "I'll be right back."

As Ms. Schmidt passed, Mrs. Rosa called me over.

"Is that your boss?" she asked.

"Yes."

"She's a bitch" she whispered.

"You have no idea" I responded.

She smiled and said, "Have a good day baby."

I smiled back and strutted outside. As I approached Radio City Music Hall, two blocks down, I couldn't believe what I had just done. I just walked out on the job. Although I could just turn around and go back, I made a conscious decision not to in spite of uncertainty. Was I having a quarter-life crisis? Or was I having a mental breakdown? Irrational was it? Probably so but whatever it was, it felt pretty good. Walking down the street seeing everyone having lunch, reminded me that I hadn't eaten. I stopped at a street vendor and got a hot dog. After paying for it I noticed that I was low on cash. Immediately I realized it was Thursday (payday). I headed up the street to the bank to check on my direct deposit.

I withdrew a hundred dollars because I imagined that I'd be doing a lot of drinking when this so called wave of liberation wears off and the depression of being jobless in a recession sinks in. Still I felt I deserved to treat myself, to some degree, especially after gathering the courage to do what I did. But on the contrary, I couldn't help but feel as if I were ditching school for the first time and was bound to suffer the consequences later.

I passed by a new bar that had just opened up earlier this week. Many of my co-workers that had gone there for happy hour raved and carried on about how great their cocktails were. The patio was uniquely decorated with adjustable glass tables and chairs made of wicker and cast iron. From the outside, I observed the low hanging chandeliers although it remained dim throughout. Calm jazz music cascaded from the opened windows—making the place even more inviting. I debated whether or not to enter—glancing at my watch as if I had some place to be.

Suddenly, a hostess wearing a white blouse and black trousers approached me. She appeared to be of Latino ethnicity and she spoke with a heavy yet endearing accent. Her spew was the epitome of sweet talk. In a moment's time, I found myself sitting at the bar with a pint of pale ale.

While pretending to watch the muted CNN program on television, I went over different scenarios in which to tell my family and friends that I'd quit my job. Although still undecided, I kept coming back to the idea of changing my work profile on Facebook to unemployed.

I ordered a shot of scotch whiskey.

"What's the occasion?" the bartender asked.

"I just quit my job." I responded.

"Ouch, tough break fella. In that case I'll have one too."

He introduced himself as Andre. He was an older brother from Jersey that sported a short afro with sideburns. Andre was a beer connoisseur, or something to the likes of it. We sampled the newest lager on tap that was from Germany.

"There's nothing like the taste of a stout lager. Germany has some of the best tasting beer in the world" said Andre.

"I agree."

"Have you been there?" he asked.

"Germany?... Nah"

"Ah man, you absolutely have to make a trip there at least once. I was stationed there back in the 90's and enjoyed every bit of it, from the beer to the food…and I especially miss the women, if you know what I mean."

"It really sounds like a lot of fun."

"It is…I'm not sure about how much it cost to get over there now, but it's most definitely worth visiting."

"Well I suppose," I said looking down into my empty glass, debating whether or not to have another.

"Look fella, not having a job is not the end of the world. Don't sweat it too much. Just know that as long as you abide by the LLC you're doin' alright."

"Yea…wait…huh? LLC? Limited Liability Company?"

"No…Listen young man, in time you'll come to find out that life is all about the LLC. That is living, laughing, and crying" he said counting them out on his fingers. "If there's a time when you're not experiencing any of these three, you might wanna check your pulse."

"Oh okay, well I hope more so the first two than the last." I replied.

I'm not sure if I understood what Andre meant by the whole LLC motto, but there was something assuring in the way he said it so I went with it.

Shortly after I paid my tab, I walked to the train station and took my time getting on it. It felt good not to have to rush. My stop was last on the route so I had a lot of time to think about my future, but I elected not to. I got off at my stop and rather than walking home like I normally do, I took a cab.

Chapter 3

The relief I felt was short lived. Upon checking the time on my cell, I discovered a text from my girlfriend Lisa. She was reminding me of our dinner reservations at Zanthara.

Ordinarily we ate out, and especially on Fridays, but never made reservations; unless of course it was a special occasion, but which one? It wasn't her birthday.

Definitely wasn't mine. No gift-giving holidays at the beginning of November. *Think, think, think…* I pressured myself. It has to be our anniversary, right? But then again there's no way I would remember that. Regardless it has to be something important. I thought it to be necessary to bring a gift just in case. But no ordinary gift would do if I were to bring about the bad news of me quitting my job.

The time now was four o'clock. Seeing that the mall was 20 minutes away in the opposite direction of the restaurant, there was no way to achieve this during rush hour. I had to think of something, and quickly. I began playing the guessing game:

Ooh tickets to a Broadway show!
What the hell am I thinking? She hates musicals and so do I.
Well maybe a concert! Nah still wasn't big enough...

Ten minutes later, my brain was exhausted from all of the guessing; and I hadn't even gotten dressed yet. Trying to calm things, I stepped out on to the balcony and lit a cigarette. With all of this stress I was in dire need of a vacation.
Hold on, that's it! A vacation! Hell yea! Why didn't I think of that sooner?! But where would we go? She'd been almost everywhere within the western hemisphere. Wherever it was, it had to be someplace new and exciting, and clean. (Lisa was slightly mysophobic.)

Suddenly, I recalled Andre the bartender's suggestion to visit Germany. Although I wasn't so sure if it was a place to plan a couple's vacation, I remember Lisa telling me her parents took a tour of the castles in Germany when she was in college. As well as how upset she was that she couldn't go due to her having a serious case of mono.

I decided to scour the junk mail on my laptop for offers and discounts on travel. I came across a package deal to southern Germany for less than seven hundred dollars. Before proceeding, I skimmed a page on things to do in southern Germany.

According to the page they were known for their automobile makers, beer factories, museums, castles, festivals, as well as shopping malls. The trip featured was for one week in Stuttgart, Germany and included a five night stay at an above average hotel. I had to admit, it sounded like a very attractive deal. For starters, I took a German language course in college and loved German beer; and in addition, Lisa was obsessed with European fashion. A match made in heaven.

Besides if she didn't want to go I could always cancel it. [Let's face it, it's the gesture that counts, right.] I booked the trip for the first Friday of December, exactly 1 month away. I then got dressed and headed out.

Zanthara was a very trendy restaurant that specialized in Scandinavian food, though in the two times we've been here we've only tried the salad. Lisa brought me here on our second date. Apparently, I screwed up by taking her to Captain Ray's Seafood Dock on our first date where she hurled at the sight of crawfish in her salad. From that point on, I was no longer allowed to pick the restaurant.

Upon entering the restaurant I received a text saying that she was pulling up to the spot. For once, I had arrived before she did.

When I first met Lisa she was interning at the C. L. Gates Convention Corporation. The following year she was hired there as a Sales Associate. Two months later she was promoted to manager, and now receives quarterly bonuses three times my pay check. I mean she was the perfect sales person; a twenty-four year old petite Jewish girl from Hartford Connecticut and a recent graduate of Princeton University. Her body was very slim and she quite frequently used her charm to get whatever she wanted. I sometimes wonder how it is that I'm even with her. She's allergic to cats and dogs so naturally she never came to my place, and I'd only been to hers twice. The only time we really saw each other was out in public or at a hotel. My brother swears out she's cheating on me; yet on the contrary, his relationship was the exact same but less glamorous. [If that even makes any sense]

On several occasions I can recall Lisa bragging about how jealous her colleagues get when she shows up with me at networking events. Was I trophy boyfriend? In the middle of my thought she walked in.

"Mel, why haven't you gotten our table? Is there a problem?" She asked.

"No, no problem, I just figured I'd wait for you so that you wouldn't have to search for the table."

"Don't be silly I wouldn't have to search, I made the reservation." She then walked pass me and gestured to the hostess. "Excuse me…I have a reservation for two under Lisa Silver."

It was rare that she greeted me with a hug or a kiss, but no greeting at all? No hi, hello, or anything. That's just rude. She walked at a very quick paste as if she was in a hurry to sit and eat. I figured, like me, she'd had a rough day. I pulled her chair out for her as she took off her trench coat. She immediately opened the menu before I could sit. The server walked over with a basket of fresh bread. Lisa hated bread.

"Oh no, we won't have this. You can take that away but before you leave we would like to have two mineral waters and two Caesar Salads no cheese and non-fat Caesar dressing please." After obliging, the waiter walked away slightly shocked.

"So how was your day?" I asked.

"It was pretty average; I had to attend the Colonial Wine Mixer this afternoon and I ended up winning the company a multi-million dollar account. Later this evening, I have to accept the Carnegie sales person of the year award."

"Wow, that's fantastic! Are you excited?"

"Thrilled" she said in an un-thrilling tone.

"So this is a celebration dinner, right?"

"What? Of course not, we make reservations here all the time [by all the time she meant once a year]. I wouldn't celebrate anything here."

"So you just wanted to get a bite to eat before going to the award ceremony?" I asked.

"Uh yeah, I didn't have time to eat lunch and you know how dreadful the food is at these types of events. Enough about me how was your day?" she asked while reading her blackberry.

Before I could answer the server showed up with our food. It was probably a good idea to break the news to her on a full stomach anyway.

Throughout dinner she constantly spoke to and texted her clients, which gave me a lot of time to admire the historic looking drapes in the restaurant. They had to have been over twenty feet tall. How often could you even clean something that enormous?

I imagined the amount of dust that would fall if someone were to shake 'em.

"MEL!" She startled me. "Are you coming or not?"

"Where?"

"With me to the ceremony… I need to know now so that I can have Cynthia reserve you a ticket", she said while cradling her cell up to her ear.

"Ummm…yeah?

"Cynthia, please reserve an extra ticket for me. Thanks"—finally hanging up the phone.

"So babe, I didn't tell you about my day" I said.

"Please don't call me that. I hate when you call me that" she replied.

"Okay, 'Lisa' can I tell you about my day?"

"Yea sure what happened?"

"I quit."

"Quit what?"

"My job!" I responded excitedly.

"Well great it's about time. That place was a complete waste of time. So where are you working now?"

"Nowhere, I just quit today."

"What? You don't have another job lined up? You're unemployed?"

"Well yea, only for right now."

"Hold on…I understand that it was a shitty job, but who quits their shitty job before finding a better one? Have you lost your mind?

"Well…"

"No really, who does that?!"

"Well of course I'm going to get a new one."

"Look Mel, this country is in a recession. It takes some serious time and planning to get a good job. And frankly, I don't have that kind of time to wait for you to get a job!"

"Huh, what do you mean you don't have time to wait? Hold on…are you breaking up with me?"

"Listen Mel, you know the type of work that I do, and how important my image is. I can't very well go around with an unemployed boyfriend on my arm in front of my clients."

"What the hell? Oh, okay so I am a trophy boyfriend?"

She began putting her trench coat on as she got up from the table with a look of pity on her face. I was outraged at the fact that she didn't answer the question. She then opened her purse and left ten dollars on the table.

"I'm sorry, I have to go," she said.

I couldn't believe what'd just happened. Talk about kicking a man when he's down. The server, right on cue, then dropped off a sixty-one dollar tab and two mints. *There goes my cab fare.*

To top off a shitty evening it began to rain, drenching me as I moped to the subway stop. On the train ride home I started to rethink things. Maybe Lisa was right. Perhaps I had lost my mind. I was twenty-seven years old with no sense of direction for my life. I'd brought this on myself.

And as for the basis of our relationship, I suppose that deep down I was hoping that in some way her brilliance would rub off on me; besides it wasn't too bad being a trophy boyfriend.

Chapter 4

The next morning I woke up to the most irritating bark from badass #1 and the most obnoxious whine from badass #2. Although I'm against animal cruelty, I wouldn't mind having one of those shock collars right about now.

I rolled over to check my phone. Surprisingly there were no missed calls from work, but I did have a new voicemail from my mom. She left a message to remind me to get fitted for my tux tomorrow. My mom was the self-appointed planner for Jeff's wedding, which was to occur mid-summer of next year.

I gave the dogs some slippers Jeff had left in my room, to chew on so they'd shut up. On the table I observed a note he'd left. It said to leave my portion of the rent on the counter and to take the dogs for a walk.

Wow I was starting to like being jobless. It gave me time to do the things that I never wanted to do in the first place. At the moment I was struggling to figure out why I felt like shit.

Hmm...I didn't drink much last night, and from the looks of it I got at least 10 hours of sleep. Oh yea, Lisa broke up with me. Nah, that wasn't it either.

After several minutes of scratching my head, it dawned on me that I purchased those plane tickets yesterday. I searched about the room for the flight details in order to cancel it.

Upon viewing the printed out itinerary, I discovered that I'd booked the wrong date. It was for this Friday—as in today. The flight was set to leave this evening. I scrambled to find my cell phone in order to cancel them before it was too late. I dialed the number and spoke with a sales rep., who must have been having a rough day because he was being a real prick over the phone. Because I didn't get flight insurance he was only able to refund me for one of the tickets. The hotel offer included in the trip was completely non-refundable. [That's what I get for buying on impulse]

I stepped out on the balcony to smoke a cigarette. The neighborhood was calm and quiet (well at least for New York anyway). After heavily weighing the pros and cons of actually going on this trip, I came to the conclusion that I needed to get away from NYC as soon as possible. My life was depressing. After all, I had absolutely nothing to do; it wasn't like I had a job to go to. Moreover, it was a nice day for flying. Without further discussing it with myself, I packed my luggage with the necessities and left my rent check on the counter on my way out.

Upon arriving at JFK via train, I checked my bags in and picked up my boarding pass. I then stopped at one of the stores and bought a magazine, a pack of small cigars, chewing gum and some pills to help me sleep. The flight time on the ticket, was a horrifying 8 hours, which is way too long to be up in the air. I boarded the plane but not before praying. As the plane began to ease on to the runway and prepare for takeoff, I started thinking to myself that maybe this was a bad idea. But either way there was no turning back now.

I read my magazine for much of the first hour until we started to experience turbulence. At this point I reached in my bag and pulled out a few sleeping pills. Clearly I'd underestimated the effectiveness of those pills because the next thing I remember is the pilot saying that we have arrived at London Heathrow Airport. The time was now 8:27 am.

I woke up having to piss so badly. As soon as we exited the plane, I spotted a young American teenage girl speaking to a flight attendant about her connecting flight. It was to Milan, Italy and it was set to board in ten minutes. The flight attendant told her to tell the shuttle operators so they could rush her along. We boarded the shuttle outside the plane and headed to arrivals. I could hear the young girl's conversation with the shuttle operator. She showed him her connecting ticket. He then replied to her in a smug English accent "there's no way you're going to make that." The eager and hopeful look she once had on her face was now unenthusiastic and hopeless as she opened her cell phone and started to call her parents.

Suddenly a Scottish speaking gentleman standing next to us, that smelled horrific, asked to see her ticket. He then said "don't worry they don't know what they're talking about, you're going to make it. I've had a ten minute connect time here before and I made it."

She looked up with a few grams of hope left and in a child-like voice said "really I can make it?"

He responded, "Of course you are, just show the operators at the security terminals your ticket."

The shuttle finally docked at the terminal. As the girl skipped away with her ticket in hand, I couldn't help but think of Charlie and the Chocolate Factory. A tear almost came to my eye. But with all of this talk about connecting flights I had forgot to take a look at mine. I reached into my coat pocket to take a look. I had 30 minutes to get to my gate.

I paid a quick visit to the restroom upon getting to arrivals. Afterwards, I ventured towards my gate. The airport was fucking enormous! I walked the moving sidewalks with haste in an effort to prepare for the unexpected. I passed the bottle check point and started up the crowded staircase. When I glanced over I saw the young girl skipping up the deserted escalator next to me. She had a huge grin on her face and yelled "I'm going to make it! I'm going to make it!" [Before it was cute, now it was getting to be obnoxious]

Ten minutes later, I made it to the peak of the stairs and found myself in the longest security check point line ever. It was set up like a maze and there was no sign of progressing. I felt as if I were waiting to ride the Avalanche coaster at Adventure Land. Next to this line I spotted an empty no wait line for preferred customers. My flight was now boarding and set to leave within twelve minutes.

Starting at the bottom of the escalator was a group of guys carrying instrument cases. They wore black p coats like mine, but with the collar turned up. I looked down at my ticket and had an epiphany. I turned up my collar and walked over to the guy carrying the guitar case and asked him a few questions about his band; this quickly turned into a conversation as we walked. When we got to the beginning of the no wait line we flashed our tickets to the guard and kept walking. Ironically, we were boarding the same flight to Stuttgart, Germany.

The plane was definitely a lot smaller than the one I boarded in the states. Luckily it was a three hour flight.
Yes, an aisle seat!
As I approached my seat, I spoke to the gentleman sitting near the window. He was reading some sort of soldier's manual. He was dressed in U.S. Army fatigues and resembled an older Jean Claude Vandamme with a buzz cut. He introduced himself as Phil and then went back to reading his smart book.

The middle seat between us was vacant, and I hoped it stayed that way. After putting away my carry on, I looked up and saw a tall and skinny blonde-haired girl board the plane while talking on her cell phone. She was walking towards me. With the majority of the plane already full, I could only assume she was going to sit in my row, and she did. She smiled at me with a sigh of relief as she approached. I stepped aside to let her in.

"Okay mom I'll call you when we land"…she said as she hung up her cell phone.
From her deep southern sounding accent I could tell she was American and not British.

She introduced herself to me and Phil the army guy as Sharnay from Indiana. As the plane prepared for takeoff, I noticed her clasp tightly on to the arm rest.

When the plane finished its ascent, I felt a strong need to break the awkward silence.

"So Sharnay, why are you flying to Germany?" I asked

"I'm going to visit my boyfriend. He's German but he lives in the states now. He had to go back home to fix some type of machine. He's an engineer and since his job is keeping him here for two months, he thought it'd be a good idea if I fly out to visit."

"That sounds nice."

"Yeah…by the way I love your hat. When I saw you I was telling my mom on the phone that I was okay because I was sitting beside a Yankees fan."

"Oh so you're a Yankees fan too?"

"Hells yeah! I got the actual Yankee Stadium seats in my apartment. They were hella expensive but I love 'em. What brings you to Germany?" she asked.

"Uhhh going to see some friends" I hesitated. (I mean who vacations in Europe by themselves?)

"Ah sweet. Do we get free alcohol on this flight? I don't like to fly so much. It's only my second time. Heck, I've never even been out of the country before today."

"I don't like to fly either. To answer your question, I think we get a choice of a complimentary beer or wine with our meal" I replied.

"Good, I need something strong."

When the flight attendant came around we ordered two small bottles of Jack and a beer for Phil.

Sharnay told us the story of how she graduated from college, got a waitressing job, met her boyfriend and became a blues and jazz singer. Although she was only a year younger than me she was living an interesting life to say the least. When I told her about the type of work I was in, ironically, she expressed how much she envied me because I had a "real" job. Candidly, I couldn't help but to envy her. I missed having a part-time gig, getting shit-faced with my friends, sleeping in late, and doing it all over again the next day.

As we talked, the alcohol continued to flow. Our first round had quickly turned in to 2 cups of wine, 6 beers and 3 small bottles of Jack. Sharnay and I debated with Phil on why the New York Yankees were America's team and why Boston blows. In our inebriated state, we made several toasts to the U.S. on a plane filled with a majority of Europeans; at the time it made perfect sense.

I took a glimpse at my watch, and noticed that we were just an hour into the flight.

I returned my attention to notice Sharnay's hand rubbing my leg while she spoke with Phil. As her hand inched closer up my thigh, I heard my pants unzip before I could even conceive what was going on. Anxiety met excitement all at once spurring a familiar sensation, yet not quite the one I was expecting. All of the drinks I consumed were beginning to work their way out. I promptly called a time out for a bathroom break. My quick steps down the aisle to the back of the plane came to a screeching halt, when I was met with two long separate lines for the lavatory.

Several minutes later I returned to my seat wondering what damage I had done in upsetting the mood. To my surprise she was slumped down in her chair unconscious. Phil was also asleep, up against the window side with his smart book tucked firmly in his hand.

An hour passed and the plane had begun its descent to land. Sharnay finally woke from her long slumber. She looked up and smiled, quieter than before and seemingly a lot more sober now.

"Are we here already?" she asked.

"Yea we're about to land now", I answered.

"Hey Mel, do you mind staying with me for a while? I'm not so sure of where to go or anything... and my boyfriend won't be here to pick me up for an hour or so" she said while stretching.

"Sure I don't mind. Although, I don't know how much help I'll be. It's my first time here too."

We exited the plane and walked through customs. She insisted that we hold hands to infer that we were together and therefore wouldn't be separated. Customs was a synch; a hell of a lot easier than when I flew to Jamaica for Spring Break last year. Hmm...perhaps it wasn't every day that a black guy flew from the U.S. to Jamaica.

While waiting at the baggage claim, I observed what looked like my bag on the other side of the conveyer. For some odd reason or another it was covered in blue chalk. I dusted it off and walked back to where Sharnay had been waiting.

She wasn't there. A few more planes had arrived, so now the area was over-crowded with passengers. Maybe she thought I'd left and decided to leave too. Or perhaps she was somewhere asking for assistance. I searched all over, then debated whether to leave or not. There was a glass partisan separating the baggage claim from the rest of the airport and she was nowhere in plain sight on the other side of it. After, about 5 more minutes of looking through the crowd for her, I decided to leave.

Chapter 5

I walked outside where several cabs awaited. I hopped in the back of a Volkswagen cab and told the cab driver to take me to the Intercity Hotel. Luckily the hotel wasn't too far from the airport because it was freezing in his cab. There was no heat yet he had a tricked out stereo system. I thought to myself damn cab drivers are cheap. I paid him 30 euro to ride for 6 minutes. So far, not much has changed from being in the U.S.

We pulled up to a historic looking hotel just up the street from a train station. The hotel lobby was smaller than I expected but with pleasing décor. I noticed that there didn't seem to be any people around that were even close to my age. Perhaps I should have booked a stay at a hostel or a Holiday Inn.

Notably, the people at the front desk were polite and spoke English. The room was standard yet cozy considering the low rate I booked it for. I looked at my iPhone and noticed that it was going on 9 pm. Now that I had arrived safely I updated my twitter to inform people of my location, just as a safety precaution. *What to do next?* It wasn't like I knew anybody within a thousand miles of here. I was going to be here for at least a week. Perhaps it was time I make some plans. I went down and grabbed a bunch of tour information from the concierge. The pamphlet on touring the beer factory caught my eye. It should definitely be worth the visit. *What would I be doing if I were back home?* Hmm...I'd probably be kicking back with a beer, eating nachos and watching football games. But then again that would defeat the purpose of coming here in the first place. Besides, there was no way they'd be showing football here. I decided to walk down to the bar just in case.

It was an old wooden tavern with random pictures on the wall that represented Deutschland. It was quite empty. There was only one older couple chatting at the end of the bar. I walked over to the counter and ordered a jack and coke. The bartender was an older guy that acted very feminine. I could hardly understand a word he was saying. He gave me a glass the size of a beer mug for 8 euro. I was starting to like Germany. I sat and watched soccer on TV for a while; it wasn't long before I found myself inebriated out of my mind. I had finished the entire glass. Hardly able to keep my eyes open, I managed to stammer back up to my room. This, in addition to the jetlag had really worn me out.

    The next morning I woke up to not only the sound of an airplane but a train as well. All in all, I guess you get what you pay for. Still, it wasn't too much of an inconvenience because I wanted to get an early start on touring. I got dressed to take my first steps out into the city. I researched the beer factory and got the walking directions on my iPhone prior to leaving. As I walked the cold and windy streets of Stuttgart, I noticed how there were several people walking in a hurry just like back home. I arrived at the beer factory just in time for the tour. The tour was pretty interesting. They offered fourteen different brands. The most popular brew was the Pilsner, of which there were free samples to go around.

Outside the beer factory I reached in my pocket for a Black & Mild cigar and lit it. It was rare that I smoked cigars but I'd always heard that European cigarettes didn't even come close to the ones in the U.S.

From afar I could see a group of three younger white guys standing together. Every so often they would look back at me and then start chatting with each other. I got the feeling that they were plotting something. My paranoia kicked in and all I could think was please don't let me have shank one of these kids. Suddenly one turned around and walked towards me. He stopped to face me and uttered some German very fast. The only word I recognized was *feuer*, which meant fire in English.

"What?" I answered out of habit.

"Oh you speak English. I was not sure if I was saying the right words. My German is not so good. May I borrow a light for my cigarette?"

"Oh okay yea sure."--I gave him the lighter. "So if German is not your language where are you from?"

"I and my brothers come from Italy."

"Oh really," I took a step back.

"The good part...Rome" he quickly added.

"Oh."

"We are on break from the university. You are Americano, no?"

"Yea I'm from New York."

"Oh, you're from New York City? –he grinned while taking a puff of his cigarette. New York, I have cousins there. It is a big city."

"Yea it's pretty big, but so is Rome I've heard."

"Yes of course. You know, my brothers were looking at your cigar and thought maybe you were smoking ganja.

"What?"

"Yes they like to smoke um…weed. You know like Bob Marley."

"Yea I know", I responded with a WTF look on my face. "Sorry, I don't have any weed."

"Well, thank you my friend. By the way my name is Nick."

"Good to meet ya', I'm Mel" – firmly shaking his hand.

He went back to join his brothers. I thought to myself…college, now those were the good old days. Damn it! Why did I have to graduate!? Oh yeah that's right to be the corporate world's bitch. What a rip!

Nick came back over and asked me if I knew where the nearest train station over here was. I gave him the name of the street across from my hotel, on which it was located. Imagine that, I hadn't even been here even 24 hours and already I was giving directions. I was headed back there any way so we all walked back down the hill towards the station. He introduced me to his brothers, Frank and Massimo. They wore a lot of Prada and Gucci sport clothing. Like all of Europe, it was like a fashion show. I took a glance at the Gap shirt I had on and I couldn't help but to feel a little bummy. As we walked they began to talk about the women they'd met at their hostel since they'd been in Germany. Giving thought to it, I hadn't met or even seen that many near my hotel. They said they were headed to Amsterdam.

"What part of Germany is that?" I asked
They told me it was in the country of Holland, about two hours from here. All this time I thought it was in Germany. A lot of my friends talked about going there when I was in college; if they'd said it was in Germany I'm pretty sure I just took their word for it. After all, that was the time I

went through my experimental pot smoking phase.

The Italians were going to Amsterdam for a day and returning tomorrow, and invited me to come along. While thinking about what I had planned, I looked around and noticed the dark cloud-filled skies. It would most certainly put a damper on things if it were to rain.

I told Nick that I would join them so I went up to my room and grabbed my passport. I checked my Twitter and noticed all the responses to my update. My cousin tweeted that my mom was mad as hell that I didn't call her. In all the excitement I had forgotten. Hell, I also forgot to take the puppies outside before I left. I'm pretty sure the messages my brother left have something to do with them pissing in the crate. Oh well.

"Alle an Bord!"—"All aboard!" When the train departed it felt as if I were on a plane taking off down the runway. They don't call it the bullet train for nothing. I began to learn more about the Italians. For example they were all one year apart, Nick being the oldest, then Frank, then Massimo. Their parents owned a few furniture stores in Rome. In a twisted way they kind of reminded me of the chipmunks. Nick was average build, and appeared more confident than the others, Frank was tall and Massimo was short and chubby.

Somehow Frank and Massimo managed to get back on the subject of marijuana. For the next two hours I sat and got educated on every type of weed there was. Although, I was already familiar with hydro, kush, haze, midgrade, and the broke man's all-time favorite... Reggie. I was convinced that they had to be majoring in botany at their university. They explained to me how to grow and cure it, small contraptions on how to smoke it, eat it, ways to hide it, and how to sell it. What they couldn't explain in English, they drew diagrams of. After the first half hour I started to regret coming along for the ride. Meanwhile, Nick chose to sleep for most of the trip.

Chapter 6

Finally, we arrived in Amsterdam. I was starving; I hadn't eaten anything since I had arrived in Germany. We stopped at a café that advertised burgers and falafels on the outside windows. It was 4 o'clock and we were the only customers there. The place had pictures of images from all over the world hanging on the wall. Some of them were of celebrities that had visited from decades ago.

We sat down at a booth and right away everybody started ordering. I was craving a burger. I noticed that the Italians were ordering weird stuff. Food I've never heard of. I assumed it was Italian. I opened the menu to find something to drink and to my surprise everything was made with weed! I observed how their faces lit up with joy.

Nick looked up from his menu and said…"When in Rome you do as the Romans do!"
Frank followed, "and when in Amsterdam, do as the Dutch do!"--waving a Dutch Master's cigar in his hand.

They started with the first few items in the menu and went down the list. It wasn't long before I joined in, under the old impression that second hand smoke is worse than first hand. *Damn you peer-pressure, you win again!* They wanted to try everything. The café started playing a Bob Marley song and they went crazy. You would have thought that Bob came back and shook their hands. Massimo was in the corner, focused on making a smoking contraption with his papers. It appeared to be a cross from rolling papers. Upon finishing it, he lit the three ends of it and took a drag from the fourth end. They all took turns passing it around. By this time, more people had filled the bar which added fuel to the fire so to speak. A haze of smoke filled the room causing it to hotbox (weed term). Before I knew it I was blown, or as the hippies say stoned. Nick got up and approached a table full of girls that wore similar uniforms—at the moment I was too high to remember what they're called. He asked one of them to dance. Frank quickly followed suit while Massimo remained in the corner meticulously packing a cigarette box with several rolled joints. I pulled out my cell phone and before I knew it I was chief tweeting (as opposed to drunken texting, when you get drunk and start texting; you get high and start tweeting). A pretty blonde haired girl with a doll face wearing a KLM uniform came up to me and asked me if I wanted a cigarette. There was always something alluring about women that smoked; something that hinted danger. Nevertheless I was drawn to her out of curiosity.

Ironically cigarette smoking wasn't allowed in the café so I followed her outside.

"American I see."

"How'd you know?"

"Lucky guess."

"Well yes, I'm from the Big Apple."

"What's that?"

"New York."

"Ah New York City…

"Yea, have you been there?"

"Yes we have flown there many times, but we never have time to do anything. I am a flight attendant" she said tugging at her uniform.

"Ah yeah I noticed."

"So you come to Amsterdam to get high with your friends huh?"

"Not really...that was they're plan I just came along for the ride. I'm more of a drinker."

"Ha ha ha"

"What's so funny?"

"You don't look like the drinking type", she uttered in her Dutch accent.

Now feeling somewhat insulted I asked "So what is the drinking type supposed to look like?

"Most of the men are chubby and have dirty mouths."

"Oh really, so I take it you don't drink."

"Why do you say this?"

"Because from looking at you I can see that you don't quite fit that description either."

"Who said I didn't have a dirty mouth?" she smirked.

She tossed her cigarette butt and while locking her eyes with mine, slowly walked towards me.

"American, I'm Melu what is your name?"

"My friends call me Mel."

"Mel and Melu, I like the sound of this" she said with a devilish grin.

In a slow and sexy tone she asked—"Can I be your friend…Mel?"

"Well, Melu…I sure hope so. Can I buy you a drink?"

"You seem to be very sure of yourself Mel."

She smiled and leaned in towards my ear to whisper "let us see how sure you are when I drink you under the table".

Cajoled yet puzzled by her American clichés, ultimately I took it to mean she was challenging me to a drinking contest.

I tossed my cigarette butt and took her by the hand.

The next morning, I woke up on a living room floor in the midst of what seemed to be a trashed condo [completely assuming it wasn't this way before I got here.] I was lying next to the Dutch girl that I had met last night, not able to remember her name at the moment. She was sleeping in shorts and a tank top. My head was pounding and I had skunk breath. Nick and his brothers came tiptoeing over.

"Mel, come on let's go" whispered Nick.

Although I was curious as to where I was and what happened last night; I was more curious as to why they were all smiling so hard. I threw on my shirt and jacket and made sure I had my cell phone and wallet.

As I turned to wake the Dutch girl, Frank interjected "shhhhh….no it's alright…we have to go" he whispered.

We quietly tiptoed out of the condo. I had no clue where we were but I did know it was pretty high up. We took the elevator down to the lobby from the 22nd floor.

The second we walked outside I was blinded by the sun. It was the brightest I'd seen it since I had been in Europe.

"So why were you guys smiling so hard? What's going on?" I asked

"We trash that place last night" Frank answered while chuckling.

"So…and…"

"It was this girl's parents' place. They called and I answered the phone" laughed Frank. "They were sooo mad and they said they were calling the police, so we leave."

"You guys are crazy. What the hell did we do last night?"

"Mel, you don't remember? Tell him Nick."

"You challenged that girl to a drinking contest. She almost beat you, but she wouldn't drink the last shot so you took it."

"What were we drinking?"

"You drink everything!"

"What?" I replied, completely oblivious to what was going on."

"Yes, and you kept yelling "I AM A FUCKING BEAST" and then you pass out on the train."

"What train?"

"The Thalys train."

At that moment I realized that we had to be in another city. In the middle of me asking where we were, I looked up to notice the Eiffel Tower in the distance.

"Nick, why in the hell did we come to Paris last night?"

"The girls invite us back to France. You don't remember anything do you? Here look see…Massimo took pictures."

From the looks of the pictures I definitely had alcohol poisoning last night. My eyes were overly glazed and I had taken my shirt off.

We stopped at a McDonalds outside the train terminal. I'm convinced we stopped there because they thought I'd want to eat American food, but at that moment I didn't care.

While biting into my Royal TS cheeseburger it hit me. "Melu! That's her name! Right?" I shouted out with confidence. "Shit, I didn't even get her number."

"Mel...forget about her...don't worry there are plenty of women in Europe. Trust me... I have a new plan" Nick responded.

"So what's the plan?" I asked, more concerned about my luggage being back in Germany.

"We go back to Stuttgart for a birthday party."

"Oh yes, le regazze!—the girls" said Massimo with excitement in his eyes.

"Huh? What's that?"

Massimo leaned in closer as if to let me in on a secret.

"Okay, before we go to the beer factory yesterday we meet two girls from the German Academy in Stuttgart. They invite us to a birthday party for tonight. Nick has the number from them. You coming, right?" asked Massimo.

"Yea I'll go, but I have to get back to the hotel and shower first."

After a long restless train ride in which my hang over constantly faded in and out, we finally arrived back in Stuttgart.

"Hey Mel, we will come to your hotel around 20. Okay man?" said Nick as we exited the train station.

"What does that mean?"

"Sorry, I mean 8 o'clock."

"Oh okay good, just call my phone."

The train station had an unseen exit that was literally across the street from my hotel, and from the distance I could see that they were quite busy today. The driveway in front was overloaded with cabs. And even the bar was encumbered with patrons. The time was now 5 o'clock and I wanted to get a quick nap in so I hurried up to my room. Everything in my room seemed to be intact and just the way I left it. Although it felt sweltering hot like the inside of an Ugg boot. In an effort to expedite the cooling process I set the thermostat to 40 before carefully choosing my outfit for the night. Afterwards, I rested on the bed and in no time I was zonked out.

Chapter 7

I awoke from the pulsating of my phone. I looked to see who was calling me but it was just my alarm. As I turned over on my side I felt a stream of sweat beads run across my forehead. Certainly, I remember turning the heater down before I went to sleep. Taking a closer look at it I thought to myself it must be broken or something. Suddenly, it occurred to me that they used Celsius this side of the hemisphere, so in actuality I was turning the heat up. I went in to the bathroom and took a cold shower. Cold showers ranked high upon my list of not so favorite things to do, but at that moment it was the most refreshing shower I'd ever had. Without hesitation, I got dressed to head down stairs; I had to get out of that room.

As I unsuccessfully tried to connect to my Twitter account, I got a call from Nick. He and the gang had just pulled up outside. I was in the bar at the time so I told them to come in for a drink but, understandably, they were more eager to get to the girls' place.

Walking out through the revolving door of the hotel, I observed Frank hanging out the window of a dark grey Mercedes as Nick blew the horn to get my attention.

"PAESANNN!!!" they yelled from the car windows.

"Where in the hell did you guys get this car from?" I asked perplexed.

"We rented it earlier; hop in so we can go meet *le regazze*!"

I got in and Massimo offered me a joint (I assumed it was smuggled from Amsterdam).

"No thanks, I want to actually remember this night", I replied.

Frank handed me a huge bottle of cheap vodka and pulled out a map to show Nick how to get to the girls' place. The girls were in a town 20 minutes east of us called Waiblingen.

After driving around in circles for about 30 minutes, we finally found the autobahn. I gave Frank a 3-6 Mafia cd to put in. To my surprise, they liked it. Massimo looked high as hell. I was a little buzzed too and hyper from the vodka. I told Nick to punch it to 150 km. He did, and we nearly passed our exit. Momentarily, we arrived at the girls' place that was located in a heavily wooded neighborhood.

In the trunk of the car was a viscacious amount of libation; the good shit too. These guys really came prepared. Eager to get a glimpse of what they looked like, I helped Frank carry some of the drinks in. They opened the door and greeted us with hugs and cheek kisses. There were five beautiful girls, all wearing short skirts and stilettos. Nick introduced me as his American brother. They were quite tall and thin with model frames--typically not my type, but gorgeous nonetheless. I assumed they were all German. They shared similar Teutonic facial features. Light colored eyes, thin lips, profiled noses, and pale skin. I could also tell they were apart of some sorority from the likes of their apartment decor. Frank and I put the alcohol on the table in the dining room. There was some sort of techno music coming from the living room. I could only assume this was the 'pre-game' to something bigger because the house wasn't quite set up with anything celebratory besides party cups and alcohol.

"Are we going to be the only guys here?" I asked Nick.

"I think so, we drink now and then we go to the party. It's not far from here."

Massimo turned and asked if he could listen to my cd. I told him I didn't care, so he went to retrieve it from the car.

Sara, introduced as the birthday girl, came over to me and asked if I wanted to drink with her.

"Most definitely" I replied.

We started out with a few shots of vodka and reluctantly I moved to beer.

During our drinking session, I quickly established a conversation in which we discussed her friends, school, and life in Germany...the typical things a girl likes to talk about.

"How long are you here from America?" she asked.

"I don't know... a night; two nights maybe" I answered in an attempt to insinuate some urgency upon the situation. "My friends and I have busy schedules, but altogether, there's no place we'd rather be tonight than celebrating your birthday with you." The more I drank the more bullshit started to flow from my lips, and it actually worked.

"Aww you are so nice Mel" she replied as her face became rose from blushing.

Massimo came in and gave the cd to one of the other girls to play. Just as soon as the first song came on, all of the girls came in to the living room singing the lyrics. I thought I was in the fucking twilight zone for a second.
I was astonished and baffled.

"Do you listen to this?" I asked Sara

"Oh yes we love 3-6 mafia," she replied.
Damn… it was evident that tonight was going to be an interesting night, presumably.

Frank reached in to one of his bags in the kitchen and pulled out a strange looking bottle. Whatever it was, he poured it in to small cups and passed them around, which everyone else happily accepted. Apparently I was the only one that wasn't aware of what it was. The cups contained a thick green liquid that smelled like Vick's Vapor rub and liquorish. Frank straddled a silver spoon on his cup and placed a sugar cube on top as he poured water over it. I tapped Nick on the shoulder… "What in the hell is this?"

"It's absinthe drink, but don't worry it's not the real kind" he answered.

I had seen the drink before in the liquor stores at home but never thought to buy it because the box looked kind of weird. Sara passed the spoon to me. I thought to myself, *yea fucking right*—I shook my head declining.

"Come on…big baby. Grow some fucking balls! Frank yelled.

"Lose some fucking weight," I recanted.

"Please for my *birtsday*," Sara pleaded.

"Okay, okay, alright already."

Not wanting to be a downer, and not to mention having the whole room focused on me, I threw it back and down the hatch it went leaving a liquorish Nyquil flavor in my mouth.

"*PAESANNN*!!!!" shouted Frank, followed with cheers from the girls.

"COME LET'S GO!!!" …shouted Sara while laughing at the bitter face I was making. She then took me by the hand as we headed out. I could already foresee that tonight was definitely going to top last night's pandemonium; but fuck it you got to live a little, right?

Everyone loaded in to the cars. Subsequently we followed the girls to the club. The route consisted of a bunch of sketchy back roads through desolate wooded areas. Finally, we arrived in a more urban setting that consisted of street lights and small stores. As we turned the corner of a side street we pulled in to a gravel parking lot.

The club looked very grim on the outside, like an old cotton mill or a meat factory. It was one of those clubs where you couldn't tell if there was anything going on in the inside or if it was a club at all. This had to be a techno club. As we entered Sara said something to one of the bouncers, who was the size of a pro wrestler, and kissed him on the cheek. She then grabbed my hand and led us all in. My instincts were right. It was indeed a techno club, with neon strobe lights everywhere. Most of the people here were dressed in tights, ripped clothing and wore glow lights around their necks. I was severely confused because the girls we were with weren't dressed this way at all.

As I walked towards the bar to get a much needed drink, Sara came up and took me by the arm and said… "Mel, come we go upstairs." We walked up the side staircase to an upper level where they were playing hip hop music. This room was much larger and had even more people in it. As we walked in they were playing an old yet classic Jay-Z song from the Dynasty album. For a second, I thought I was back in New York. There was a familiar aroma that filled our side of the room. I looked around and standing next to me was guy smoking a black and mild cigar. Now I truly felt at home. Nick and I followed the girls to a table on the mezzanine, while Frank and Massimo headed to the bar. They came back with bottles of champagne and beer. The waitress then brought flute glasses and yellow shots in plastic test tubes.

"They're called piss shots! You must try one", said Sara.

I stood aside with my beer and watched as the rest of the group downed their piss shots toasting to Sarah's birthday. The girls chatted and danced with each other while we stood at the rail overlooking the dance floor.

Nick leaned towards me and asked… "So which one do you want?"

"I hesitated…It really doesn't matter they're all beautiful."
He looked back and confirmed "you're right about that my friend; I think the birthday girl wants you to come over."
I turned around to look at her; she was winking and signaling me to come over with her index finger. I walked towards her with a smug smirk on my face. As I approached, she put a mint in her mouth. I took her by the waist side and almost instantaneously, yet unexpectedly, her lips pressed up against mine followed by the coolness of her tongue. Some way or another I ended up with her mint. Oddly, it tasted pretty stale for a mint. I had to take another swig of beer afterwards. Suddenly she pulled me by the shirt and said "come let's dance!" I turned to the guys and told them to come with me as she pulled me along.

We proceeded to the dance floor and as for some odd coincidence, as if someone shouted USA's in the house, the DJ began to play all of the latest chart topping songs from back home. After the first few spins he started to incorporate some fist pumping songs. *Ok, now things were starting to appear more realistic.* As I observed people on the dance floor, I saw that there weren't any good dancers here. In fact they were pretty bad; but unabashed to admit it, so was I.

The dance floor, which was fair before, was crazy packed. The DJ played a popular German song, which I actually recognized from the 90's that everyone shouted the words to. They proceeded to jump up and down and pump their fists. People from the balcony began spraying champagne in to the crowd and the waitresses started to dance in iridescent cages located on both sides of the bar. The music continued to thump louder and louder. It was if the whole club had gone mad and I surely expected Euros to start falling from the sky at any moment. The excitement overwhelmed us all. I looked down at my shirt and saw that it was soaked. I couldn't tell if it was from sweating or the champagne.

As I clawed my way from the dance floor I felt my heart beating faster than usual. I then touched my forehead. I was burning up in temperature, even hotter than previously in my hotel room. I walked back down stairs because I remembered passing some restrooms on our way in. Although my vision was blurred my main concern at that moment was to get dry. I knew that from the time we left the girls' place, the temperature outside would have dropped to freezing by now.

Luckily no one was waiting in line, so I dashed in to the bathroom in search for a hand dryer but found paper towels instead. I took my shirt off and rang the sweat from it. Glancing in the mirror I could see that I was perspiring all over the place. My vision had grown fainter and I began seeing small spots as well. Someone must have put something in my drink. I definitely had to go lie down somewhere. My first thought was to get the keys from Nick so that I could go lay in the car.

I exited the bathroom only to enter a crazed techno world, which by now, was annoying the hell out of me. The lights tormented the little eye sight I had left, to the point where I couldn't see where the hell I was going. Looking down at the floor made me feel like I was in the fun house at Coney Island. When I stood still everything started to spin and for a moment I felt sick. Slumped over in the hallway, I refused to hurl because I knew exactly what would follow…more hurling. I stood up with the back of my head pressed against the wall and my eyes closed. The coolness from the wall started to relax me and my heart rate finally eased to a normal paste. Just to be sure I was ok I stood there for about twenty minutes. I would have stood there even longer but a song with tremendous bass started to vibrate the wall, giving me a pulsating headache in return. Upon opening my eyes, a tall skinny girl with red hair wearing a pink latex skirt walked by and randomly squeezed both of my cheeks. She then skipped along towards the dance floor. *WTF!?* I had to get the hell out of here. I pushed off of the wall and walked up the steps to find the guys.

The club seemed to be a little bit calmer now and I could see Massimo on the balcony at our table. I staggered through the crowd and made it up the top of the stairs, then headed towards the mezzanine. There was a crowded line filling the stairway, and in the distance I could see Massimo smoking in the corner. I leaned over the side of the rail and hollered out to get his attention. He spotted me and came over and held out his hand to pull me up pass the crowd. Back at the table, I took my wet shirt off and put on my coat.

"Where's everyone at?" I asked. While sipping his beer, Massimo stood at the rail and pointed down. Right as I looked down, the entire place was in a fucking panic! Everybody was running to the middle of the floor as if there was a fight. All I could hope was for it not to be Nick and Frank. As I zeroed in to the center of the dance floor, low and behold it was the Italians. Nick was on the ground choking someone and Frank was being pinned down by a bouncer.

Against my better judgment, I rushed down the stairs. By the time I got to the fight Massimo was already there wrestling with a guy beside Nick. He had to have jumped from the balcony.

My vision was still blurred but I managed to see someone jump on Nick's back. I came from the blind side and swung as hard as I could. At once my fist connected with a face bone, perhaps fracturing my hand on impact. I came back to swing with the other hand only to miss because the subject had already fallen to the floor. As I started to kick him I got swiped in the side of my head with a bottle. It wasn't hard enough to break the bottle but certainly hard enough to hurt like hell. While on the ground trying to recover from a slight concussion, I started to cough extremely hard and found it difficult to breathe. I take this as someone must have sprayed pepper spray. Suddenly, one of the bouncers grabbed me by the back of my coat. I squirmed out of it and hauled ass following the crowd making their way to a side exit. My heart was beating even faster than before. When I came darting out of the doors not only was it freezing but it was raining as well. To my left, which is the opposite of where everyone was running, I spotted a tall girl with long dark hair. She stood underneath the fire escape smoking a cigarette, and resembled Sara from behind. As I started towards her, my sight grew dimmer and my legs got weaker.

"SARA!" I bellowed out before collapsing to the wet pavement.

Chapter 8

    I slowly opened my eyes to the brightness of the sun spreading throughout an unfamiliar living room. Again, I had absolutely no recollection of how I got there. One thing for sure, it felt like I had been drugged. My head was pounding and my nerves a bit shaky. My right hand had been wrapped snug in cloth bandages. I couldn't tell if the pain in my back was from the fighting last night or the couch that I was sleeping on. Faintly in the background I could hear a familiar tune playing, but with German lyrics. I turned to lay on my side with my eyes half squinted to see the television. It was the theme song from Sponge Bob. To my surprise, there was a little kid knelt in front of the TV drinking out of a mug. She was pale skinned with short brown hair; around the age of 8 or so. She laughed uncontrollably as she watched. As my mind tried to piece things together I kept drawing blanks. I didn't feel as if I were in a threatening environment so I stayed calm and tried to rationalize things. First, I remember going to the club, partying with girls, fighting alongside the Italians, then running out of the club; the rest was all a blur.

I quickly examined my body to see if I had sustained any other injuries. Aside from a sore hand and a headache I was fine, but immediately after that I realized I had on someone else's clothes. I was wearing an extra small shirt with a cartoon printed on the front and small running shorts. As I looked around the room for my clothes I started to panic. Maybe someone had stolen them. My wallet, passport, money as well as my phone were in my jeans.

I didn't want to disturb the kid from her cartoons, but I needed some answers. As not to startle her, in a low and calm voice I uttered *"Guten morgen"*—"Good Morning." She turned around and looked back at me with a smile and said *"Morgen* Papa!" —"Morning Papa!" and then went back to watching her show.

"Papa?" I repeated.

I looked around the room and no one else was there. I thought for a second. Never have I known papa to be a German word. My mind was in a blitz trying even harder to recall the events of last night. Could I have adopted a kid? Not possible that late at night. Could I have gotten married to her mother last night? Possible, but I had no ring on my finger and I doubt I would have slept on the couch afterwards. The only reasonable explanation is that she was confused and I was lost.

"Hey little girl…um where are your parents?" She turned and smiled and said something really fast in German. Apparently she didn't speak English. "*Was ist Ihr Name?*"—"What is your name?" I asked.

"*Mein Name ist Emily*"—"My name is Emily"…she answered.

"Okay, *mein Name ist*"—"My name is" … Before I could respond she yelled "Papa!" then smiled.

The door began to rattle. Someone was about to come in. The little girl ran upstairs as if she was afraid of whoever was on the other side of the door. I looked around for a back door but didn't see one. Before I could even sit back down, the door opened. In walked a slightly older Caucasian woman; approximately early thirties. Her hair was pulled back with a hair band, while a few pieces hung to her chin. She was carrying a bag of potatoes. Perhaps the little girl's mother, I assumed. She remained at the door and looked at me, with her captivating hazel eyes, as I stood helpless and confused near the sofa.

"Hallo. How are you feeling?" she asked.

"Umm....I-I feel okay. So…where am I exactly?"

"You are in Haslach, about 10 miles south of downtown Stuttgart. You fell and passed out outside of the club last night and I brought you here."

She took a look at the television and without hesitation, yelled "EMILY"!!!!!!!!!
Emily ran down the stairs and the woman spoke German to her. Emily made a pouting face as if she had gotten in trouble.

"I'm sorry I told her not to wake you" the woman said.

"That's alright she didn't wake me. But um…I was kind of looking for my clothes?"

"Close? Excuse me, I don't understand."

"My clothes…like my pants and stuff."

"Oh your clothes, yes they are drying. They were wet so I dry them. Come, I can get them for you."

I followed her into the kitchen and sat at the kitchen table. I still had so many questions because there were still so many blanks.
 "Is your husband here?"
 "No, I'm not married."
 "Is your boyfriend here?"
 "No, I'm not with a boyfriend."
Her answers were short and I wasn't exactly getting the extra feedback I wanted. Perhaps I was asking the wrong questions. I continued.
 "What is your name?"
 "Hannah" she replied as she began to fold the clothes from the dryer.
 "My name is" …before I could answer she said "Mel right?"
 "Yea how'd you know?"
 "I saw your id in your wallet" she replied, holding it up for me to see.
 "Oh okay; is Emily your daughter?"
 "Yes she is."
She handed me my jeans as well as my cell phone and wallet and sat down at the table.

89

"Emily called me Papa. Do you know what she means by that?" She sat at the table with her face resting against the palms of her hands and gazed at me with a smile. She chuckled.

"I don't get it what's funny?"

She pointed at me and in a calm voice said "your shirt…you have papa Smurf on your shirt. You didn't have on one last night so I gave you this one to put on."

I took it off and looked at it. *Oh wow what a relief.* I then put my shirt and pants on and sat down to face her.

"I really do owe you a great deal of gratitude for what you did. So thank you very much Hannah. If there's anything I can do to repay just you let me know."

She smiled slightly and said "you're welcome and don't worry about it".

"If you don't mind me asking, how old are you?"

"Here it is not polite to ask a woman her age", she responded with a cold look on her face.

In an attempt to quickly change the subject I asked her if she worked at the club.

Consequently, she was there last night checking on some arrangements she'd made with the club. I also found out that she worked as a nurse at a hospital in Stuttgart. In the middle of conversing my stomach began to growl.

"Are there any restaurants or fast food places nearby?" I asked.

"Oh, I'm so sorry how rude of me. Are you hungry?"

"Yes, but I won't trouble you. You've done more than enough already."

"No you will stay here and eat with us. It is no trouble."

Hannah prepared a great deal of chicken soup. Emily hardly touched her food, and there was plenty left over. She urged me to have as much as I wanted. The hunger pains I felt would've easily caused me to over indulge, and I didn't want to give off the impression that I was greedy.

"Your phone rang while you were asleep" she said.
I took a quick look at it and saw that I had seven missed calls; all of which were from Nick. I excused myself from the table to call him back.

Nick answered with a bit of urgency in his voice.

"Hey Nick what's going on?"

"We couldn't find you last night when we left the club. Are you okay?"

"Yea somehow I ended up at this lady's house but I'm alright."

"Good, the *Polizia* were everywhere; we thought maybe they arrest you."

"No I'm fine. How's everybody else?"

"Good, well kind of. We are just leaving the hospital. Frank broke his hand last night."

"Damn…where are you guys headed to when you leave the hospital?"

"To the airport we have to go back home."

"You mean back to Italy?"

"Yea we just wanted say goodbye. We leave tonight."

"Well I doubt I'll be back in time to see you guys off. Tell Frank and Massimo it's been fun." Before I could finish saying goodbye, my phone dropped the call. In the middle of scolding my service provider, I noticed there appeared to be water coming from the sides of it. Last night's rain must have gotten a hold of it somehow. My battery was dead. I had to get back to my hotel ASAP to charge it. I returned to the kitchen.

"Hannah, I need to get back to my hotel. Is there a bus or train station near?"

"Yes there is. Just a minute please, I will show you."

"Okay, thanks."

As she walked upstairs the doorbell rang.

"Mel that is my sister, can you let her in please?" Hannah yelled down.

Chapter 9

I went to open the door. There stood a gorgeous petite young woman with long dark hair and piercing green eyes. She had an olive skin complexion similar to Hannah's. Early twenties I suspected. I hesitated in amazement. She stood there and smiled at me, followed with "*Guten Taq*"— "Good Day".

I recanted "Hi…umm…Hannah's upstairs."

"Okay, I am Inga and you are?"

Before I could answer, Hannah came down and gave her a hug as they started chatting in their native tongue.

"This is Mel, a friend. Mel, this is my little sister Inga."

"Nice to meet you" said Inga while shaking my hand.

I responded with *"Ver suchen Sie"*—"Nice to meet you".

She and Hannah both looked amazed.

"Ah sprechen sie Deutsche?"—"You speak German?" Inga asked.

"A little bit, just a few phrases here and there" I replied.

Emily came thundering down the stairs "INGA!!!!" she screamed while running up and hugging her.

Hannah turned to me, "are you ready Mel?"

"Um, ready for what?" I replied.

"You want to go to the train station, no?"

"Oh yea, but if you point me in the right direction I can find it myself. Your sister just got here and I don't want to burden or further inconvenience you."

"Melll" Hannah said in a low motherly tone while cutting her eye at me.

"No. You will come with us," Inga happily insisted. "We will have lots of fun right Emily?"

"Yaaaaaay!!!" cheered Emily.

"Well if you insist", I responded while shrugging my shoulders.

"Let's go Papa," joked Emily.

"I hope you don't mind, we have to make a stop downtown" said Hannah reaching into her purse.

"Oh no, not at all" I replied with an insisting smile.

As we headed to the bus stop I couldn't help but notice how similar this was to having a family outing. I made sure to pay close attention to the process of taking the bus as I knew how expensive taxis here were. The bus fare had to be paid in advance at a ticket machine near the stop. All of the buses had a touch pad for opening the doors upon entering and exiting the bus. These buses were a lot bigger and a lot cleaner than the buses I was used to in New York. Hannah told me that the majority of people in Stuttgart take the bus and the train as appose to driving because of limited parking. I felt this was quite ironic considering it was one of the most premier automobile makers in all of Germany.

When the bus arrived downtown, I was surprised to see so many people out shopping on a weekday. The store outlets were numerous and resembled a market place. As Hannah entered a department store, Emily started to pull Inga's hand and begged *"Ich mochte einige Eis"*—"I want ice cream".

Inga smiled at me and said "I'm going to take Emily to get some ice cream. Want to come?"

"Sure."

As I walked with Inga we began to get to know each other a little. She was twenty-five years old and lived in Koln Germany, but was visiting Hannah due to a fall break from school.

She was somewhat skeptical of how I knew Hannah and also curious as to why my hand was bandaged. I told her the story of the previous night all the way up to the point when I met her today. Initially, she was taken aback by everything but still viewed me as a guest.

"Mel, do you eat ice-cream?"

"No thank you, I'm alright."

"How long will you be staying in Germany?" she asked.

"Just for a couple of weeks or until my money runs out" I joked.

We walked back up the way to meet up with Hannah. She was leaving the store just as we approached. She seemed to be in a disturbed mood. I could only wonder what was going on as she and Inga spoke discretely. Inga must have discovered my perplexity from the look on my face.

"They want to charge her 200 Euro for a scarf for Emily" Inga said.

"Wow! That's a lot of money for a scarf."

"Yes it is. But don't worry we go somewhere else" she replied.

"Mel, what hotel are you staying?" asked Hannah.

"I'm at the Intercity Hotel."

"We can walk with you if you'd like."

"Sure, it's right up near the train station."

Up at the hotel, I could see that everything was back to its sluggish pace. Inga and Hannah decided to wait for me in the lobby while I ran up to my room. Upon examining my room, it had been cleaned and my bags were just as I left them. Most importantly nothing was missing. The temperature was now back on burr; what a relief.

Seeing that it was my last day as a registered guest, I headed back down stairs to extend my stay and join the others.

It was starting to get late and seeing as they had to hurry to catch the bus, I bid farewell to them. I also thanked Hannah for all that she had done for me and exchanged numbers with Inga.

Afterwards, I rushed up to my room to charge my phone. In about an hour or so it started to work again, with the exception of being able to check twitter of course.

I took a moment to reflect on my trip thus far. What kind of purpose was I looking to fulfill here? I couldn't really say that it was a trip for rest and relaxation. Hell, from the moment I stepped in to Europe I'd done nothing but party and bullshit. It was time for me to either get focused or just go home.

That night was only the second night I slept in a bed in the four days that I'd been here. It felt great sleeping in the next morning too.

Right as I was about hop in the shower, I got a text from Inga. She and Emily were coming this way for lunch and she wanted to know if I wanted to join them. Seeing as I hadn't scheduled anything, I agreed.

A few hours later, I spotted Inga and Emily standing outside a Mexican restaurant called La Hacienda.

"Halo Papa!" teased Emily.

"Halo Sponge Bob" I teased back.

Inga seemed happy to see me.

"How are you? She asked.

"Ser Gud und Du—Very good and you" I responded.

"Auch Gud Danke—Also good thanks" she replied while smiling.

The hostess approached and showed us to our table.

"So where is Hannah?" I asked.

"She is working today."

"Oh so you're just out spending some quality time with your niece huh?"

"Yes, we go ice skating today" Emily interjected. "Mel, are you coming? Please! Please!" Emily pleaded.

"Sorry I don't ice skate, but I don't mind watching the both of you."

"Oh come on", said Inga. "You have to skate too!"

"Mel, I can teach you" insisted Emily. I can skate really good.

"You can skate really well"…Inga corrected her.

"Okay, maybe I'll give it a try. But I'm not making any promises." I responded.

During lunch, Inga asked me lots of questions. A tad bit more than I was prepared for. She inquired about my family and was very intrigued in what I did for a living. I neglected to mention how I quit my job. Instead I chose to share with her my lifelong dream of becoming a writer.

Inga, an overachiever from what I'd gathered, was extremely fascinated with this. She continued to inquire; this time more earnestly about when and where I write, what I preferred to write about, as well as whom I was interested in writing for. Not wanting to purposely avoid her questions, I had to be quick on my feet. I told her that I would most likely write about sensitive and serious issues. And that as a reader, I enjoy stories that tend to leave more of an impact on morals and ethics.

She hung on to every word as I carried on. To me, it was a wonder to have an attentive listener as Inga.

Lisa never listened to me at the dinner table; in fact I can hardly remember ever being able to get a word in for that matter. She would constantly ramble on about how someone or something was annoying her at work, or how much business she was getting for the convention center, and tons of mediocrity. Recalling the night we broke up, I never even got the chance to tell her about the tickets to Europe.

Although, I can't say I didn't see the break up coming. It was bound to happen. We rarely spoke on the phone and our sex life was virtually non-existent. Frankly, I was more hurt from not having a job than her breaking up with me. Nevertheless that chapter was over.

"So Inga, do you like to travel?"

"Oh yes, all of the time. Honestly, there is not much to do here in Germany because the weather is cold and rainy all year round. Most German people work and save up throughout the year just to travel and vacation. I, myself, have been all around Europe and Asia but never to America."

"Ah that's a shame," I added.

"I very much want to go to New York and California. Everyone here talks about vacationing in the states" she added.

"Well those are definitely popular destinations. Hey, I have an idea! If you don't mind, could you show me around a little bit? And if or when you come to the states I could show you a few places as well?" I asked hoping she would say yes.

"Sure. Where would you like to go?"

"I would like to see historical places. I minored in history when I was in college and I think it would be an interesting subject to write about. You know, just to start out. I've been thinking about writing about the changes in European culture over the years; Germany, to be specific."

"Sure. That's a good idea. We can go to the tourist center near the train station tomorrow. Is that okay with you?"

"Yes, that's perfect, I responded."

After lunch we walked up the block to the outdoor skating rink. I stood in line behind a short black man who spoke English. He was getting a pair of ice skates for a little boy that I suspected was his son. The man wore a green flight jacket and beige combat boots. I assumed he was stationed here at the U.S. military base. He reminded me of Andre the bartender from back in NY.

"Come Mel, put on your skates," said Emily tugging on my jacket.

"I'm not sure about this, I could break my ankle," I said to Inga.

"Come here you baby, she said tightly strapping the skates on to my feet."

We slowly walked on to the ice and right off the bat, I fell down. It was as if I'd never skated in my life. I used the toy penguin (training wheels for beginners) to stand up.

Emily quickly skated over and was determined to teach me how to skate. Meanwhile, Inga began to show off her skills by doing a series of twirls. I noticed a smirk on her face. She came slowly gliding over until suddenly she fell, ass first, on to the ice. I tried my best not to laugh. Instead I reached down and helped her up, then handed her the toy penguin. She laughed hysterically.

After an embarrassing and painful lesson, it was getting late so I walked with them to the subway station. Upon entering the station, I got a strange craving for croissants. This was credited to the bakeries that filled the terminal. I was used to the subway stations smelling like brake dust and piss.

    We sat and waited for their train. Emily, worn out from the fun-filled day, fell asleep in Inga's lap. Inga and I began to make plans for the next day. Not before long, the train approached and I bid goodbye to them. Inga told me that she had a fun time and, surprisingly, placed a single kiss on my cheek.

    The next day Inga met me out in the downtown square. She brought a map that she'd gotten from the tourist center along with her. It labeled all of the nearby museums and historical sites in all of Stuttgart.

Our venture began on a small tour van that circled around the entire city. The tour guide only spoke German, so poor Inga had to translate everything he said. From what I gathered, this southern part of Germany sat at the for-front of industrial and agricultural innovation. It was home to the Mercedes Benz and Porsche museum. The city took pride in their home grown produce, wines, and beers; but above all their soccer team. Shortly after the van tour we viewed the Porsche Museum, and then famous relics of art at a nearby art gallery located just off of the autobahn.

The art gallery was very still and quiet as the two of us were its only visitors at the moment. The majority of the works dwarfed us in comparison. No flash photography was allowed, which only made the silence even more awkward. As we walked throughout the different rooms, I'd often glance at Inga while making a silly face. She'd then burst out into laughter. I felt this was the perfect opportunity to ask her a few questions of my own.

"So Inga, were you and Hannah born and raised here in Stuttgart?"

"No not at all. We are not German."

A bit dumbfounded, I paused at her response hoping that she would clarify.

"We're from Russia. Hannah and I came to Germany with my grandmother. Our parents passed away when I was just a baby."

"Oh my, I'm sorry to hear that."

"It's ok; Hannah remembers more about them than I do. What of your family in New York?" she asked.

"Well, I have one older brother, Jeff, who is studying to be a doctor and my mother is a florist. As for my father, I never really knew him…he and my mother had a big argument one day and he left. She never bothered to look for him and he never bothered to call; that is, according to Jeff. I was just 3 at the time."

"Oh I am so sorry to hear that" said Inga.

"It's cool, shortly after that, the three of us moved further up state to live with my grandparents. Do you have any more family here in Germany?"

"Yes we have a few cousins, but they're all crazy."

I laughed.

"No I'm serious, they're really crazy… and they hate German people. Hannah was like them too at one time. She ran away from my grandmother's house when she was seventeen and we didn't hear from her for years."

"We thought she had gone back to Moscow, but she was just hanging around the streets of Germany. Eventually, one day she just showed up at the house pregnant, and with her new husband."

"Husband?"

"Well ex-husband now…Emily's father Gino. My grandmother hated Gino. He was so disrespectful, and a drug dealer too. He caused my sister a lot of stress you know. All the time he was in and out of jail.

"Is he in jail now?" I asked.

"No, he has been out since four years, maybe five. But he now owns two clubs outside of the city. I really don't like him; he rarely comes to see Emily. He is so full of shit, you know."

I could see that Inga was getting upset from the escalation in her tone of voice. As soon as there was a pause I planned on changing the subject; but she beat me to it.

"I'm kind of hungry from all of the walking around. How about you?" she asked

"Yea sure, I could eat."

"What would you like? There is pizza, Chinese, Mexican, McDonalds....."

"Well, I haven't been to any German restaurants since I've been here and I'd hate to come all this way and not try any German food."

"Hmmm let me think, she pondered. There aren't many good German restaurants downtown. They're east of Stuttgart in Bavaria."

"How far is that?"

"It is about a two hour train ride. Hmm I know! I can cook for you. Would you like that?"

"Yea sure, I don't mind that."

"Okay. We can stop by the grocery store on the way to Hannah's."

The grocery store was much like the grocery stores in New York small and compact, except they had no grocery bags. Not even for purchase. Luckily, Inga's purse was big enough to fit everything. While waiting for the bus, she showed me how to purchase a bus ticket from the machine as well as how to read the schedules. She also taught me how to count my change. I pulled out the coins I had in my pocket. The whole time it hadn't occurred to me to count it. I had about fifteen Euro worth of coins in it.

Since I'd been in Germany, I often noticed homeless people meticulously rummaging through waste baskets and recycling bins carrying big plastic bags. Inga informed me that they were in search for bottles. Apparently, five bottles were worth one Euro. I was amazed upon discovering this. Even the homeless had jobs here.

We arrived at Hannah's house. No one was home. I gathered that she was at work and Emily was at school. I sat down and watched television as Inga got started on dinner.

Moments later Hannah and Emily walked in. Hannah quickly spoke to me as she headed in to the kitchen. Emily ran up to her room with her head down. I could only wonder what was upsetting her.

I could overhear Hannah and Inga having a conversation in German, which I couldn't decipher. Although, I heard Emily's name come up quite often.

Inga walked in to the living room to tell me that dinner was ready and yelled for

Emily to come down. The dining table was nicely prepared. Inga had prepared veal chops and pasta called Spatzle along with salad and bread. As we all sat down to eat the phone rang. Hannah got up to answer it. She excused herself from the table and walked in to the living room.

"How is the food? You like?" Inga asked.

"It's super, you did an excellent job. Where'd you learn to cook like this?"

"Mostly from my grandmother and Hannah, she answered."

Shortly Hannah returned back to the dinner table. She appeared less disturbed than before. She spoke off and on to Inga in German while glancing at me and Emily a few times. I understood very little.

"Mel, we have a favor to ask of you", Inga said. They both looked at me.

"Sure what is it?"

"We were thinking that since you were good at English and writing that maybe you could help Emily with her lessons."

"You mean like a tutor or something?"

"Yes, a tutor" Hannah answered. "Just for a few hours in the week, I will pay you."

"There's no need for that, I will do it for free. Surely it's the least I can do; especially for all that you've done for me."
The both of them thanked me. In addition, Hannah thought it'd be more convenient for me if I stayed here in the guest room upstairs. Even though I'd already extended my stay at the hotel until Saturday, I had no problem with it. At least I would be closer to Inga.

Later that evening, Inga told me that Hannah had been under a lot of stress lately and she couldn't understand why Emily had been getting bad marks in school. Emily's father hadn't been of much help either. They were afraid that the separation was starting to affect Emily's concentration at school. On top of that, Hannah was needed to work longer shifts at the hospital. Luckily, Inga was there to help out.

Chapter 10

Hannah gave me a few of Emily's English lessons. I skimmed through her textbook to find there were supposedly two versions of the English language, the UK version and the American version.

We started off with a reading lesson. I had her read a paragraph written in German and subsequently another written in English. To my astonishment, she read both correctly and at the same pace as if it was easy to her. She then turned to focus her attention on the television.

"Emily, did you understand what you just read in English?"

"Ummm...she hesitated [as if she would be in trouble if she said no]...a little bit."

At that moment I understood exactly what the problem was. She couldn't relate to the material. An episode of Sponge Bob was coming on. She sat Indian style on the floor waiting eagerly.

"Do you like this show, Emily?"

"Yes, I love this show."

"Would you like to take a break and watch this?"

"Oh yes please, she said excitedly."

"Alright, let's make a deal. I will let you watch this but only if I can watch it with you and it has to be a secret okay?"

"Okay", she nodded quickly.

"But my German isn't so good, so you have to tell me what they're saying. Deal?"

"Deal!"

Throughout the show she translated so much that she hardly had anytime to laugh. For the next few nights we continued this as our tutoring lesson.

Her next exam was scheduled for Friday. That Thursday night I wanted to make sure Emily was prepared. I had her read the paragraph written in English from the first night. The paragraph was about a little boy named Paul and his friend Thomas. It described their experience at the library. First I showed her how to identify the subject in the sentence, then the nouns. Next, I had her identify the verbs. I then, replaced Paul and Thomas with more familiar names such as Sponge Bob and Patrick. Instead of describing the library, I had her describe their day at the Crusty Crab (Sponge Bob's job). We then went back and described the library. She discovered that she had used a few of the same words when she'd described the Crusty Crab. We continued with these exercises for a while and then I let her do the rest on her on. She got the majority of them correct.

The weekend had arrived and I had become more accustomed to life here in Germany. Public transportation was routine at this point. I was able to get downtown, to Emily's school, to the train station, as well as to the airport on my own. Through my observations around town, I recognized that the people here pretty much kept to themselves. At times when I felt the need to stop and ask for assistance, the younger people were more eager to provide it.

Hannah and Inga wanted to take me out to dinner as a thank you for tutoring Emily. They told me to dress nice because it would be a surprise.

I walked Emily over to the neighbor's house to spend the night with her friends. When I returned, the girls were all dressed and ready to go. Inga looked stunning in a floral printed white and silver colored gown. Although, I'd have to say Hannah looked ravishingly as this was my first time seeing her with her hair let down. Her lustrous curled locks drooped over the side of her right shoulder down to her black and white striped dress—which she wore so well. They both stood tall and sexy in high stiletto heels. [There was no doubt in my mind that I was going to have to fend off the wolves tonight.]

Instead of taking the bus, like we normally did, Inga drove Hannah's car. It was a green BMW, 2001 740i to be exact. I sat in the back while Hannah prepared her makeup in the front seat.

We arrived shortly at a big glass building. After taking the elevator up to the top floor, I was eager to see what this place looked like.

It was a nice tapas restaurant with a live band that played Arabic music. I was so amazed to see a place this welcoming here in Germany. Everything was like a scene from a movie. The dim atmosphere was complimented with a view of downtown and the hills of the neighboring subdivisions, which was much like Van Gogh's *Starry Night* painting.

"So Mel what do you think?" asked Inga
"This place is very impressive" I replied.
"Yes, they have the best live music in all of Stuttgart. Are you hungry?"
"Yea, sure"
I took a look at the menu and not too much to my surprise I couldn't understand a damn thing. I really needed to brush up on my German. I looked up from the menu to see Inga smiling at me.
"Don't worry I will order for you. You like steak right?"
"Yes, that's perfect."
Shortly after ordering, the waiter brought out a basket of fresh baked bread that smelled way too good to turn down. Unaware of such customs, I decided to not be the first to reach for it.
"Would you like some bread?" Inga asked.
"Sure, thanks."

Hannah happily helped me choose a bottle of wine to go with dinner. Notably, I'd never been treated with such kindness. If there was anything I could say these were definitely my kind of people.

After consuming a superb dinner, the unexpected happened. Inga asked me to dance with her. I was nervous to say the least but the wine was kicking in by this time. I escorted her out to the dance floor. The band had just begun playing a slow song. Out the corner of my eye I could see Hannah laughing at the two of us. Inga had a smile on her face as well. The heat quickly began to rise from the pressing of our palms. Her hair swayed in the air as I gave her a gentle spin. Her scent smelled of fine essential oils. Towards the end of the song she planted a soft kiss on my cheek. I smiled, and in the back of my mind I was desperately hoping that this was fate attempting to repair my broken condition; starting with my love life.

"Wow, it's really warm in here, yes?" said Inga, fanning the brim of her blouse.

"Yea, I suppose it is. Would you like something to drink? I can pick something up from the bar."

"Sure, can you get me some water please?"

"Sure, I'll bring it to the table."

I went to the bar, which was very crowded by this time, and ordered a few waters and another round of drinks. When I returned to the table I was surprised to see a man sitting in my chair, facing Inga. He wore a brown leather jacket. As I walked closer I could see that he was around my age. He had dirty blonde hair, a pointed nose and very big eyes that were cloudy and red as if he was sick or something.

"Here is your water, Inga. I ordered another round of drinks so it should be right over."

The guy sat there staring at Inga with an awkward smirk.

"Mel, this is Klaus," Inga said with a stern and irritated look on her face.

The guy didn't acknowledge that I was even there, so I didn't speak to him. Instead, I was concerned about Inga and what was going on.

"Is everything okay?" I asked while looking at Inga. Her face was stone and her voice silent.

"Nice to meet you I am Inga's boyfriend" he said finally breaking his silence yet making the situation even more awkward.

I looked back at Inga for confirmation— nothing. She neither confirmed nor denied any truth to his statement.

I then responded "nice to meet you"--slightly dazed and confused.

"I am sorry, am I in your chair?" he said.

"No that's fine, you can sit there. I'll pull up another one."

I pulled up a chair next to Inga. "Where is Hannah?" I asked.

"She went to the restroom" said Inga.

"Mel, how do you know my Inga?" he asked.

"He is a friend of me and Hannah, Inga interrupted.

"You sound American, what brings you to Germany?" he continued.

"He's writing a novel and doing important things with his life," said Hannah upon returning to the table. "Now what brings you here Klaus?...Besides stalking my sister."
Still a bit confused and trying to get a better understanding of the situation I began to ask questions of my own.

"So Klaus, how long have you and Inga been dating?" I asked inquisitively.

"Five years at the next month. We live in Koln together."

"No, we used to live together," interrupted Inga again. "We have been on a break" she said with fury in her tone.

I could sense that Inga was embarrassed by his unannounced presence.

Klaus moved closer to Inga and began speaking German way too fast for me to understand anything he was saying.
He then pulled a small box out of his pocket and kneeled down beside her. He opened the box, exposing a ring. I could only guess that he was in the midst of proposing, as I saw Inga's eyes light up followed by a huge gasp.
She nodded her head, too speechless to say anything. Simultaneously, I felt sick to my stomach. She hugged him and they began to kiss surrounded by the applause of a few tables near us who had been eavesdropping.

I, myself, was confounded in yet another "WTF?" moment. Hannah displayed a look of disgust on her face and then stormed away from the table. I told Inga that I would go check on her, but I doubt she realized due to her preoccupancy.
I caught up with Hannah just outside on the terrace. She had a cigarette in her mouth as she dug through her purse.

"Allow me." She leaned in to me as I lit her cigarette, then mine.

121

"Can you believe this - this shit!?" she started.

"No... I can't...I had no idea Inga had a boyfriend."

"I just don't see why she would even think to marry this S*tupo*!" said Hannah with frustration.

"I take it... you don't like him?"

"No! Of course not, he is an asshole! This asshole is a spoiled brat and a drug addict. He spends all of his parent's money on drugs. I hate him." she said while exhaling smoke.

"Ha, I can't believe it" she uttered as she folded her arms and looked away.

"Well I don't understand why she would want to be with him. Does she do drugs too?"

"Huh...my sister? No. She stayed and tried to help him. He is the only guy she's ever been with. I'm so upset with her because every time she leaves him, she goes right back. I tell her that money isn't everything; but no, she can't see that behind all the gifts he buys her" she said while shaking her head. "I am sorry Mel; I know that you liked her. I should have told you about him."

"Well, I have to admit that that didn't go at all as I anticipated, but I'm cool. Besides, I didn't exactly get the chance to develop those feelings for her"—obviously lying through my teeth.

I felt feelings for Inga the moment I saw her. It's not so clear exactly what kind of feelings they were; my libido was overbearing at the time. Nevertheless, at the moment I felt like the one guy from *The Last American Virgin* movie that couldn't get laid. Furthermore, the second she accepted his proposal I could hear that sad *Just Once* song by James Ingram playing in my head.

In any capacity, I was experiencing shortness of breath and this cigarette was doing absolutely nothing for me, except for perhaps making things worse. Honestly, I seem to have the worst luck with girls as of lately.

As I flicked my cigarette, up in the distance a firework soared across the cold night sky and then exploded in to a bright flower of red and silver fireballs. Hannah, still worked up, grabbed me by the hand.

"Come let's go!"

"Go where?" I asked.

"Don't worry, just come with me. If they can celebrate we can too, no?"

We hopped into a cab just outside the building, and took a ride downtown. Our first stop was a small café, opposite the clothing stores, that served cocktails.

"What would you like to drink? I pay for the drinks tonight okay."

I was caught a little off guard so I just agreed to have whatever she was drinking.

She leaned towards the girl behind the bar and ordered. *"Swei treffer mit Tequila bitte!* —Two shots of Tequila please!"

"Did you just order us Tequila shots?"

"Yes. Do you want something else?"

"No-no- that's fine. I'll drink whatever". (My mind said no but my half broken heart said fuck-yea!)

"We make a toast to my future retarded, coke sniffing brother-in-law. Just kidding, this is supposed to be your night. So this is to you! I really appreciate you helping me out with Emily. You will make a good father someday. Hoist!!!!!"

She signaled the bartender for two more.

"Hold on a second! Don't you think we should take it a little slower?" I insisted.

"Ah come on Mel, you can't drink with a woman?"

"It's not that, I'm just saying… I don't want to have to clean your vomit off my shoes" [protecting my ego]

"Relax. Drink these and then we will go to someplace else, okay?"

I would have never guessed where we ended up next. We walked around the corner up a narrow cobble stoned street and towards a brick building that casted a blue light outside the doors.

It was a strip club. There was no line out front so we walked right in. Hannah seemed to know everyone. They greeted her with hugs and kisses.

"What are we doing here?" I asked.

"I used to work here" she replied.

"Huh? You used to be a strip- I mean exotic dancer?"

She smiled as she waved at one of the dancers. "No, I was a waitress."

We took a seat at the front of the stage. A waitress wearing lingerie came up to us and took our order.

"Mel, what would you like?"

"I'll just stick with Tequila."

"*SWEI* TEQUILLA!" Hannah yelled over the noise.

Hannah took out a wad of cash and tipped the dancers on stage, generously. I could see she was having a good time as the black lights casted down on her face and caused the white stripes in her dress to glow.
Moments later she walked towards me with one of the dancers.
 "Mel, this is my friend Janette."
 "Hi, how are you?" Janette greeted me, wearing nothing but a silver G-string.
Janette was my complexion, tall and slender with red hair, dark round eyes, and full looking breast.
She had a long flower tattoo that ran up along her side, as well as an Ethiopian flag tatted on her shoulder. I'd have to say she was the prettiest dancer in the place by far.
 "Hello, nice to meet you" I responded; completely altering my mood.
She smiled and whispered something to Hannah. They began to laugh in unison.
 "What's so funny? I asked."
 "Janette thinks you look like Kobe Bryant."
 "Huh? Really?"

"Oh don't worry you're cuter than Kobe", Hannah replied. "Come with us to the party in the back and bring your drink," said Janette.

My curiosity grew with vigor as my mind began to ponder. Slowly my buzz started to work its way in. What kind of party could be happening in the back of this hole in the wall strip club?

The three of us continued to the back behind a dark velvet curtain. I could smell hookah smoke and Egyptian incense in the air. The lights were now dimmed red. I remained calm, but all the while I couldn't help but think that this had to be a champagne room for VIP. There were private booths with suede furniture sectioned off and adjacent to the room we were in.

Janette helped me take off my jacket as Hannah directed me to a plush white loveseat sofa in the corner. Hannah then sat cater-cornered to me in a similar, but smaller, chair and began smoking from a hookah tube.

At this point I knew that one of us would be receiving a lap dance. *So hoping it was me.*

Janette leaned over me slowly gesturing my face in to her busty bosom.

She smelled of that baby powder scented lotion that all the strippers in the states wore to cover up any odors. Her skinned sparkled with glitter specks. The song resonant in the background was a slow song that I'd never heard before, but the perfect song for Janette to slow grind to. I looked over to observe Hannah. She had now removed her jacket and sat up straight with her legs crossed. I could see a serene look of encouragement on her face through the thin clouds of smoke. She was definitely enjoying her buzz. In fact, her stature resembled a queen having her servant entertain a guest. She continued to smoke from the hookah, and watched as Janette snaked her naked body across me; placing kisses on my neck. By this time, the alcohol had transitioned itself into my system quite nicely. As I came to the point of arousal, my whack ass bladder started to send those familiar signals again. The song was nearly over, so I was determined to hold it.

At the end of the song I tipped Janette 20 Euros as I got up to go to the restroom. She smiled and gave it back to me and said hurry up back Kobe.
The restroom had a long trough-like urinal. The wall was covered in Polaroid pictures of

strippers and flyers. As I set off for what seemed to be the longest piss of my life, I began to count the pictures. I got to 34 when I came to a picture of Hannah holding a beer mug and a serving tray. Her hair was shorter and dyed red. The black lingerie outfit, she had on revealed the curviness of her body. She seemed a lot happier back then. I would have taken the picture as a souvenir, but it was too high to reach.

I returned to the so called party/champagne room. To my astonish Hannah was now sitting in the loveseat that I was previously sitting in, and getting a lap dance from two new women. I sat down in the chair next to them and fired up the hookah. The vibe was now enhanced to second gear. This was like no lap dance I'd ever seen before. They all moved as if they were on ecstasy. [If only New York was this exciting]

The girls kissed and breathed heavily on Hannah's neck while rubbing and grinding on her. Hannah opened her eyes, instantly fixated on mine. For a minute I felt the need to look away until, unexpectedly, one of the girls slid down the strap of Hannah's dress revealing one of her breast. Aware of her exposure, she never broke her lustful eye contact with me. I'd never been so inspired in my whole life. This was surreal. I had now entered the realm of voyeurism and there was no turning back. The other girl turned and looked at me with a smile on her face, beckoning me to come over. Was this my invitation to a ménage?

As I started to get up from my chair the song came to an abrupt end and I could see the regular lights come on beneath the velvet curtain in the front.

Hannah fixed her dress back and put on her jacket as she giggled and talked with the two girls.

What a rip! I guess they could see the look of disappointment on my face, which I tried to hide. I put my jacket on as we bid goodbye to Janette and the girls.

Outside, I laughed and conversed with Hannah about what a fun and crazy night it had been. She concurred, but suggested we stop one more place.

As we walked back towards the train station we stopped at the *Weihnachtsmarkt* Christmas square near the outdoor skating rink. It appeared completely different at night. The festive décor and burning

Christmas lights brought a feeling of warmth to the bitter midnight air.

Hannah had a surprise for me. She went up to the lady working at the drink counter of a small gazebo and ordered two drinks. She then handed me a warm mug.

"What's this?" I asked

"It's called *gluhwein*. That means glow wine in English. They warm the wine with cinnamon and cloves, and then add amaretto to it; try it."

I took a sip.

"Wow that's really hot!"—burning my chapped lips

"Drink it slow. It's good, yes?"

"Oh yeah it's good...and strong."

"Come we can sit over on the bench. It's a little cold out tonight, reminds me of Moscow."

The wind blew furiously, sending a chill our way and causing us to shiver and take more sips of the "glow wine". I could see Hannah's face starting to turn blue. I gestured her to move closer and stretched my arms offering the warmth from the inside of my coat. Although, she felt pretty warm as she stretched her legs to overlap mine.

"Mel I have to tell you something", she whispered low.

"What is it?"

"I'm drunk," she replied.

"Well yea I kind of figured that. We've been drinking all night," I joked.

"No, I think I'm really drunk" she laughed.

"So Hannah, I didn't know you could be so fun."

"Why do you say that?"

"You sort of act a little cavalier around me."

"Huh? What is this?"

"Well I guess what I mean to say is you're usually kind of distant towards me, you know… less warm."

"I am a nice person but I have to really get to know someone before I can…um…be open and really start to trust them. You understand me?"

"Oh okay, well that makes sense. Do you trust me now?" I asked.

"A little bit, but then again I am drunk" she laughed.

She sat her glow wine down and held on to me tighter clasping around my sides. I could feel the cold tip of her nose brush against my neck. Her alluring perfume was starting to draw me closer. Normally I would have been hesitant to make the first move, but something about the situation seemed too perfect to pass up. I slowly turned to face her and instantly her lips met mine. The kiss which started out simple and innocent grew hot with fervor closely followed by heavy breathing and caressing.

That one kiss numbed all of my senses while not only stopping the wind from blowing, but halting the cold all together. A euphoric feeling swept over me causing me to feel lighter; the feeling that only a sensible dose of morphine could give. Suddenly, Hannah stopped and looked around. She then whispered "let's go back to your hotel."

"TAXI!!!!" I shouted from the park bench. The hotel was only three blocks south of us, but I was on a time limit and if it meant blowing a few Euros so be it. Hannah was humored by my urgency but still maintained a sense of eroticism in her eyes.

The cab pulled up and the second we got in, we commenced were we left off. Things undoubtedly started to heat up in the back seat as she kissed on my neck and nibbled on my ear. Twice we had to remind the cab driver to watch the road.

At last, we arrived in the drive way of the hotel. I couldn't believe how convenient this hotel was. They could definitely expect great reviews from me on trip planner. After happily paying the fare I escorted her in. The lights were dim yet lit enough for me to find a path to the elevators.

The moment the elevator doors closed, I grabbed Hannah and released the most passionate kiss I'd ever given. It was apparent she felt the spontaneity in it all, she obliged by stripping me of my jacket and unbuttoning my shirt without hesitation. Even as the elevator doors opened at my floor we remained inside, and I continued to explore her soft lips.

The moment I stepped out from the elevator I reached for my hotel key as if to insure immediate entry. I slid the card key in the slot and got a green light on the very first try. It was definitely symbolic in the sense that everything was a go. [But even if it hadn't opened, the nearest ice machine room would have done just fine.] Hannah jumped in my arms kissing me even more lustful than before as if we both were building up towards shuttle launch. The motions caused me to fall backwards to the bed. Without delay I undid the clasp of her bra while she, impatient with the last few buttons, ripped my shirt off. I really couldn't believe what was going on. Was this really happening? At the beginning of the night, in no way had I foresaw any of this.

She whispered in to my ear "do you have a condom?" I reached in my back pocket and responded "never leave the country without 'em." As my hand inched up her dress, she stopped me.

"Wait…I have to go to the restroom I'll be right back!"

Why do girls always have to go to the restroom the moment you're about to get it on?

In the meantime I prepared the bed to look more fitting for what was about to go down. I then reached into my bag for a few spritz of cologne, not too much though. The toilet flushed.

"Oh please don't let her be sick, we need this win" I said referring to me and my counterpart.

Not one second later Hannah stepped out of the bathroom, and instantly I froze. Her body had me at attention like a soldier at war. There she stood in nothing but a white laced thong, smiling and showing her body off. Just below her thong near her hip was a tattoo of a red rose. Her tanned body shimmered in the bright bathroom light, almost making her appear somewhat goddess-like. Regaining my sight, I began to see that she had the body of a 25 year old. Her breast upright and becoming yet supple, her stomach lay flat and unseen, yet her curves mind-blowing; her legs firm and tight and to top it all off, her hair flowed loosely contributing to her overall Amazonian appearance. I rose to my feet to properly greet her with a kiss.

First, I started at her lips then slowly moved to her neck as I caressed her frame and cupped her breast with my palm. She then put her arms around me and we proceeded to the bed, where I softly laid her down. Her sweet fragrance was absolutely mesmerizing. She aroused me just from the look in her eyes. I started off patiently, feeling every part of her body as my team began to warm up.

Needless to say, I scored—several times. Every enticing look she gave me, kept me wanting more; and not for one moment did she ever give way. This remained the case for the next three hours. It was apparent that we were literally going to sex to death. Alas, I had to do what was necessary; fake a cramp injury and call a time out.

Hannah and I sat at the edge of my hotel window nestled and wrapped in a single sheet, sharing the last cigarette. We just sat there smiling at each other, as either of us hardly had any strength to move. But every now and then she would lean down and give me a kiss and tell me how bad she needed that. In all the tranquility, my mind slowly began to drift.

"What's the matter?" she asked.

"There's something I've been wondering" I began.

"What is it?"

"Why did you help me that night outside the club? I know you were there conducting business and all…but what made you decide that you wanted to help me, a complete stranger, and a half-naked passed out black guy at that? I could have been a bad person or simply up to no good."

"I'm a nurse. My job is to help people. Besides, you reminded me of someone; someone who had helped me when I was your age...

"In my early twenties, I started waitressing at the strip club at night and going to nursing school at the day time. One night after leaving the club, my girl called me to pick her up from a hotel up near Canstatt. When I got to the hotel I called her and she told me where the room was located. I waited in the car for her but she was taking a long time so I called her again. Someone answered the phone by accident and I heard her scream HELP! I went up to the room and there were three Albanian guys beating her. I told them to leave her alone, and then I began calling the police. They grabbed me and tried to rape us with the door open. I can remember screaming as loud as I could. Some people even walked by and didn't do anything. I slowly started to give up and thought they were going to rape and beat us to death. And then all of a sudden this young guy ran in the room and jumped on two of them. It was a black American soldier. His friends came following behind him and they saved us. His name was Private T. Jackson. You kind of look like him. If it weren't for his help we could have died that night. Women get raped and killed here often. Especially young women; which is why I want to get Emily out of Germany and to a nice place with good schools; somewhere in the states."

As I watched Hannah talk and open up, I felt really thankful to have met her. After all, I could have frozen to death lying outside of the club that night. As for the way tonight went, she totally saved it from being a complete bust. I was curious as to why such an extraordinary woman was still single.

"So how did you meet Emily's father? Inga told me that he was a club owner."

"Gino…he would come to my work from time to time; only to see me. At the time I was still living in fear of the Albanian guys that tried to rape us. Gino was really known here and I felt safe with him. We started to go out and one day he asked me to marry him and…I said yes. I was only Inga's age. Ha'… way too young. And like Inga, I couldn't see just how broken our relationship was."

"What do you mean by that?" I inquired.

"We were married for just two months and he was arrested for drug smuggling. I was pregnant with Emily at the time and so I waited for four years visiting him often. When he got out we tried to make things work but he wouldn't leave the crime alone. He was arrested a year later and this time I didn't visit."

"Do you still speak with him?"

"Yes we still speak, but lately he's going on my nerves. For two years I ask him for divorce. He just signed the papers last week and he has not seen his daughter in three weeks."

[And I thought my relationship was bad.] I could sense the frustration in her voice, as her English started to get a little choppy. I opted to change the topic.

"Are you working tomorrow?" I asked.

"No, I have the whole weekend off."

"Super, we can sleep in" I replied while yawning uncontrollably.

"Come, we go to sleep" she said taking me by the hand to help me up.

Chapter 11

"Wake up my sleeping beauty" said Hannah, fully dressed and sitting at the foot of the bed.

"Huh? What time is it?" I said still a bit hung-over.

"It's eleven o'clock. Good to see you're not talking in your sleep anymore."

"Wait, I don't talk in my sleep. Do I?"

"The night I brought you home from the club you kept calling yourself a beast in your sleep."

"Ohhh"...I responded looking down in embarrassment.

"But never mind, I have a surprise for you."

"What is it?"

"No, I'm not telling yet, it's a surprise. Close your eyes."

"Okay. It's not Christmas over here already, is it?"

"No, just close your eyes and open your hands" she demanded.
She placed an unwrapped box in my hands.
I opened my eyes. It was a digital camera.

"Wow. When did you get this?" I opened the box to check it out.

"A little while ago, while you were sleeping."

"Thanks." I gave her a kiss on the cheek.

"Is this so we can take naked pictures of each other?"

"Huh? Why you thinking so dirty?"

"Hey, I don't know maybe you're in to that", I teased.

"No silly, but I think maybe you will need it."

"Why?"

"We're going to Munich this weekend."

"Really? Just me and you?"

"Yep, there are a lot of places we can visit. People act a little bit different there but they have really good food."

"Awesome, when do we leave?"

"Today at noon"

"What about Emily?"

"Inga will watch her until we get back."

"So I take it you spoke with her today."

"Yes."

"And how did that go? You didn't mention…umm…you know?"

"Yes of course, we are sisters we talk about everything. Don't worry she is good. She wanted to apologize to you for last night. Oh and she said she still wants you to show her around in the states, or something like that?"

"Hmm……So everything is cool?" I reiterated.

"*Ja!* it is; trust me it is a good idea that I'm not around Klaus at this time. Me and Inga both agree."

"Alright then"

"Come let us get ready."

That day we didn't waste any time. We arrived in Munich, Germany at 2pm. The weather wasn't as cold today, yet the grayed out sky suggested rain. [Then again, it always looked that way in Germany.]

Hannah suggested that it would be a good idea if we tried the 2-day extended package that included a night tour of Munich. The tour would kick-off on the outskirts of Munich and end back in the city at The Olympic Park. It would commence the next day at the market place and then out toward the countryside.

The first site we visited was a concentration camp called Dachau. And a good thing that it was first, for I would have never step one foot near this place at night. Just the sight of the gate was eerie enough to stop you in your tracks and turn you back around.

As we approached the entrance, the wind made an awful whistle through the openings of its iron rods and barbed wire. The water surrounding the camp stood half frozen in the trenches. The grounds, enormous as they were, lay cold and barren. Outside the outer fence were backyards of a later developed neighborhood; what brave souls they were.

The closer we came to the main building I could see that everything was set up like a museum or memorial. A cast iron sculpture hovered above the dates 1933-1945. There were many scribed plaques written five times over in different languages (this goes to show the array of people imprisoned here at one point). Everyone in the tour group appeared to be desolate and silent, even the children. That is, with the exception of Hannah. She had more of an intriguing look on her face. Like me, this was her first time here as well.

The gravel shrieked from our footsteps as we walked, which made me imagine the hundreds of guards and prisoners that walked the same grounds. The more we walked and viewed the scenery, the more I started to think what an incredible waste of land this was and how depressing it was to be here. Although the camp didn't host executions it still reeked of hate and nihilism. Fortunately, this part of the tour was shortened on the count of rain.

The next part of the tour was a lot less depressing. We trekked towards the metropolitan area of Munich for the night expedition. The closer we got to the city the more the rain died down. Eventually, we ended up at the Olympic Tower. It was enormous and overlooked the city, which was perhaps five times the size of Stuttgart, and you could even spot the Swiss Alps from the observation deck. Hannah and I took a great deal of pictures of the panoramic view.

Afterwards we enjoyed a quiet dinner at a Bavarian restaurant near our hotel, before retreating to our room.

"So how is the writing coming?" Hannah inquired while turning down the bed.

"It's ok, I'm just undecided of where to start first; you know, writer's block."

"Today, I didn't see you with anything to write on. I thought writers carried a note pad or maybe a recorder."

"Well yea but…I just don't have one with me; Left it back in Stuttgart."

Hannah had an idle expression upon her face.

Rather than trying to outwit or further mislead her, I began telling her the truth about my occupation in New York in its entirety. She was a bit subdued when I finished. And of course I expected her to be upset, which was evident from the look that she displayed. She then began speaking in a tranquil manner.

"Listen Mel, I understand that you didn't know me well enough to tell me that in the beginning. I am that way myself, but I want you to know that you don't have to lie to me…"

"I know."

"Let me finish…but…I am also happy that you trust me enough to tell me that", she smiled. "I am also proud of you because quitting your job takes a lot of courage. You have to live for yourself, and if your job is making you unhappy then you must leave" she said shrugging her shoulders.

At that moment I realized that the universe had bestowed upon me something I was desperately in need of—a true friend. I'd only known her a week, and yet her sincerity and how she empathized with me was incomparable.

"You're something else you know" I said simply, then kissing her hand.

She smiled, then pressed my head to her bosom and turned the lights down as we retired to bed.

The following morning we set off early to enjoy the last part of the tour. It mostly consisted of the markets downtown and a tour of the countryside. The countryside was unlike the downtown square where people mostly hung out in cafes and smoked cigarettes, in fact there were hardly any people at all. We visited the vineyards, where Hannah taught me how to select the best wines for any type of occasion. The samples where all the more exhilarating.

To wrap up the tour, we visited two castles that dated back to the 12th century. I took plenty of pictures, but I was more interested in the people that lived scattered about in the surrounding areas. Most of them were older and lived off of the land. Not much had changed here over time, which I imagined contributed to their overall happiness. It was said that this area was known for having the longest-living people in the world. In fact, one castle was hosting a couple's seventieth anniversary; which deeply moved Hannah.

On the way back from Munich, we stopped at the Cannstatter Festival, a carnival just outside of the city. It was located in the town of Bad Cannstatt, which was home to one of the biggest distributors of the famous Stuttgarter beer. Hannah was amazingly fun. She wanted to ride every ride, from the roller coasters to the pirate ship, the Ferris wheel and even the swings. She claimed to have not been to a carnival since high school, and she vowed to bring Emily here soon.

In all the excitement, we worked up a hunger so we stopped at a food stand that sold all types of hot dogs. In the middle of eating my currywurst, I could hear a faint level of bass coming from speakers in the distance. I followed the sound, taking a couple of steps in its direction. It was coming from an enormous tent with a few people waiting in line outside of it. I assumed it was some sort of circus act seeing that this was a carnival. Hannah noticed my curiosity and asked me if I wanted to go in.

"It doesn't matter" I responded, trying to down play my interest.

"Come let's go," she said guiding me by the hand.

The closer we got the louder the music was; this time with the addition of cymbals. I noticed that the people leaving the tent had a cheerful smile on their faces. Some were even chanting songs in German. As we passed through the opening of the tent I could see that this was no circus.

This was beer fest at its best; loud music, over-flowing beer mugs, guys wearing old-fashion overalls and gals dressed in their St. Pauli girl outfits. Together, they sang old drinking songs in a drunken stupor on top of picnic tables as the band on stage prepared for their next set. There had to be over a thousand people in this tent. It was the size of a football field.

Hannah and I sat at an empty picnic table in the very back. The table was littered with a host of various drinking games. The drink menu was printed in old German so I had Hannah order for me. I felt my bladder was starting to spill over again so I excused myself to search for a restroom.

I followed the signs to the back of the tent where there stood about fifteen port-a-johns, each with lines. To the left I saw a man come from what looked like a small trailer with a curtain. Inside were several open stalls. [Perhaps some people actually liked to wait in lines.] In any event I stood there and let er' rip. At the moment it was the closest thing to an orgasm. When I got back to the table Hannah was there awaiting me with liter mugs of beer—half of hers already gone.

"Wow, how long was I gone? You were pretty thirsty huh?"
She nodded her head yes, incapable of speaking with her mouth full as she took a big gulp from her mug.

"You have to catch up", she teased.

"You do remember what happened the last time we did this", I reminded her.

"Enough talking, more drinking!"

I was definitely up for the challenge. As I removed my jacket, I thought I heard someone yell my name above all the commotion. I turned my attention towards the stage; then back the other way--nothing. I sat back down and gripped my beer mug preparing to go to work.

"MELLL!" someone shouted.

I turned around and saw a skinny blonde-haired girl walking towards me holding a beer in one hand and the arm of a male companion in the other. I couldn't believe it. It was Sharnay from the flight over.

"Hey!" She released the guy's arm to bestow a hug. "How are you? I thought I lost you at the airport" she said with a look of concern.

"I'm good…I see you made it out pretty safe without me. Is this your boyfriend?" I asked.

"Yes, this is my boyfriend Johan. Johan this is Mel, you remember the guy I told you helped me through customs."

"I love your hat man, GO YANKEES!" He shouted as I shook his hand.

I then turned to introduce Hannah, whom had a quiet puzzled look on her face. She smiled and shook their hands.

According to Sharnay, they'd just arrived minutes ago and couldn't find any place to sit. Hannah slid over and invited the couple to sit with us. Oddly, her hospitality was kind of a turn on. I smiled and sat down to my beer.

We tried our best to engage in a normal conversation over the thumping of the speakers. Hannah spoke with Johan in German off and on as I chatted with Sharnay. This was the first time either of them had been to beer fest although beer was their favorite drink of choice. In fact they seemed to be beer fanatics. They were just as enthused about beer as the Italians were with marijuana.

I could see that the conversation was starting to bore Hannah. She would give me a quaint look every now and then, glancing down at my mug to remind me of the challenge. I think she just wanted to get me drunk so that, later this evening, things would be as crazy as the first night we made love. [And there was definitely nothing wrong with that.] To shake things up and make the night a little more interesting, I got Sharnay's and Johan's attention.

"So guys, before you came in Hannah and I were just about to have a drinking contest. Are you game?"

"HELLS YEA that sounds fun", said Sharnay in her southern accent.

"Okay cool, well to make it fair we'll do co-ed teams...Hannah and I against you guys."

Hannah summoned me to the middle of the picnic table as if to tell me a secret.

"Mel, you and me are going to drink the same beer from here on, she said with a smile."

I didn't really understand what she meant, but complied anyway.

We ordered the first round and shortly everyone started off with a fresh liter of beer.

I took a sip. There was something different about this beer she had ordered us. It was less stout, but it tasted good nonetheless.

Exactly one hour later there were fifteen empty liters scattered on our wooden picnic table. The tent was spinning with excitement. Most of the excitement was from Sharnay who, at this time, was on stage trying to sing a jazz song to a techno beat. In the middle of her solo she started to

make out with a random girl from the audience.
And by now, poor Johan was in one of the various port-a-johns upchucking his dignity. (That's assuming he chose not to wait in line.) With the room looking like a bunch of high-strung kids all zipped up on pixie stix and energy drinks, I felt as calm as a box turtle; so did Hannah. She looked at me very subtly and smiled.

"Are you drunk?" I asked.

"Just a little", she replied.

"Do you want to go?"

"Sure…do you want to go?" She asked with her eyes appearing more alert.

"Yea, let's get out of here."

We exited the tent and the lights of the carnival lit up the dark night sky.

"Why aren't we as drunk as Sharnay and Johan? I asked quite puzzled. "We definitely had more to drink than they did."

"Ha, ha, ha"…Hannah began to laugh.

"What's funny?" I asked

"Nothing…" she said while giggling.

"Tell me, please I wanna know."

I began tickling her to make her confess.

"Okay okay I will tell you" she finally cried out. "Our beer was mixed with Sprite."

"Huh? Are you serious?"

"Yes," she said laughing even harder.

"So you were going to cheat if we hadn't been on teams?"

"Well just a little…but you're a man, you can handle it."

"Oh please whatever." I continued to tickle her until she screamed for mercy.

We walked back to the train station. There was at least an hour before the train to Haslach was to depart so we went to a Japanese cafe and lounge across the street. We sat in the back corner and looked on, as it was karaoke night. The beer—weak as it had been—began to stir up a little curiosity within me. I was still curious about Hannah's childhood and perhaps her reasoning behind running away from home. One by one I fired off my questions which, in this case, proved to be just as stupid as drunk dialing or drunk texting.

She told me horror tales of growing up sheltered and isolated, as well as being discriminated against in Moscow for having dark hair and dark eyes. And although she had arrived in Germany after the fall of the Berlin Wall, not much had changed as far as racism and classism went. Her reason for migrating to Germany was even more overwhelming.

"Inga was too young to remember, but our parents did not die in a car accident. My mother worked under a branch of the USSR as a government researcher from Moscow. My father was a Jewish physics teacher from Spain. Things were… how you say…tense in Russia at this time because the cold war had not too long ended. Sadly, one day they were condemned to be communist spies and were sent off to be executed.
A childhood friend of my mother brought me and Inga to Germany to live with her mother, whom we called our grandmother. Hannah and Inga aren't even our real birth names. These are typical German names so that no one would come after us."

"So what are your real names?" I asked.

"I am Onya Zukov and Inga is Vicktoriya Zukov. She is the only real family I have left."

The look on Hannah's face was very grim; it almost seemed as if she wanted revenge. I could see the water that filled her eyes refusing to be released as she gazed off in the opposite direction. Again I felt at a loss for words in light of these new shocking set of details. I quickly came to understand the rationale for her disposition. One had to be tough in order to endure such trauma at a young age.

Up until now, all of my life I've felt like I was at a disadvantage when it came to women. I felt as if I were looking into a one-way mirror. That is to say that no matter how hard I tried, I could never see beyond the glass to the actual person that was staring straight at me; observing every flaw I possessed, every imperfection, every obscurity in which I tried to keep hidden. But now I was on the other side of that mirror looking in, discerned with the intangibleness of Hannah's pain.

It was apparent now that she trusted me and deep down I valued that. So naturally, there was a part of me that absolutely hated to see her like this. It was up to me to reverse the effects of the can of worms I, regrettably, opened.

Suddenly, I had an epiphany. I knew what I had to do to cheer her up. I excused myself from the table to go to the restroom. When Hannah wasn't looking I sneaked over to the karaoke stand to sign up for a song. This was a stretch for me seeing that I was the worst singer on the planet, and highly suffered from stage fright.

I couldn't make out any of the songs in the book so I just told the karaoke deejay to plug me in to any Michael Jackson song. Looking out from the stage I counted only eight people. Now I knew I could make a complete ass of myself without hesitating. The song I picked started to play so I stepped up to the microphone and cleared my throat.

"This song is dedicated to a very special young lady named Hannah."

Hannah then looked up from her drinking glass and saw me. She had the "what are you doing" look on her face. I began singing the chorus at the beginning but as the verses started to pour across the monitor, I was lost. This had to be the one Michael Jackson song that I didn't know. I could see that I was losing her attention so I gave up on singing and tried my best MJ impersonation. From the corner of my eye while perfecting my spin on stage I could see Hannah whistling and jamming along in the corner. The crowd backed her up. She even pulled out a few Euros and waved them in the air.

As the song wrapped up I was out of breath and my crotch ached from grabbing it thirty six times.

"Good job Mr. Jackson", said Hannah applauding as I walked towards her. She couldn't stop laughing hysterically. I'd have to say, the smile on her face was absolutely worth me making an ass out of myself.

We grabbed our things and headed back to the train station. After the train departed, I noticed that we were the only passengers on our train car. I took this as an opportunity to see if Hannah wanted to fool around for a bit. To my surprise she was up for it. Suddenly the train approached the next stop and the conductor helped a young lady load her bike on from the platform. At that point, we decided to wait until the coast was clear but ultimately just ended up falling asleep.

Hannah and I arrived back in Haslach feeling refreshed. Earlier, Inga had dropped Emily off at her friend's house to stay the night, before heading back to Koln. We had the place all to ourselves, so we eagerly began from where we left off. Afterwards, I held Hannah in my arms as she slept. I was unable to, as I reminisced over the incredibly extravagant events from the past weekend.

I couldn't help but feel invigorated and my life rejuvenated. Being afforded the luxury to make love to a beautiful woman all night until the wee hours of the morning; it was unreal to me. Often, I'd felt the need to pinch myself to make sure it was really happening and not just some super vivid dream. Surreal as it seemed, I realized that somehow I was living proof that it was possible to start an entirely different life. But would it last? And if so, how long would it be before my past life caught up with me? To answer that question, not long at all.

<u>Chapter 12</u>

The following Tuesday morning, I received an urgent message. It was from my grandfather. I called him back right away, not frantic but unsure of what had happened. My grandmother had slipped and fell on some ice outside their home in Albany. She was hospitalized overnight and had just returned home. Luckily, she hadn't fractured anything. He asked me if I could come to see her. I didn't feel like lying so I told him where I was and the whole story behind it, but somehow I think he already knew.

"You know your mom has been worried about you Mel."

"I think she's a little more concerned with Jeff's wedding right now gramps" I replied. He then proceeded in one of his nobility talks, which always left me feeling guilty and foolish in the end.

"That's not true and you know it. Your mother just wants to make sure you're able to take care of yourself son. Listen to me when I tell ya that this world is somethin' else. Nobody cares about anybody out here. Everybody wants what's in their best interest. People are selfish and that's how it's always been."

"Yea, I know gramps, but...

"Mel, I'm not trying to chastise you but I'm giving you knowledge that you wouldn't obtain until you're at least forty years old."

I sighed.

"We care about you son, and that's why it's so important not to shut your family out of your life. Your family will be here for you when no one else is. I understand your frustrations about not having a job. You're a man with your own money and if you want to travel around the world that's great. You're young you should—but you don't do it like this. At least let your family know something. We worry about you because we love you." [I wanted to interject, and state that I'd left a message on twitter concerning my whereabouts—but knew better.]

My grandfather has always been a wise voice within the family. He and my grandmother practically raised me and Jeff as their sons. To hear the worry in his voice unsettled my conscious. Pressed on seeing me in time for Thanksgiving, he offered to pay for my flight back home. But out of guilt, I couldn't accept it. Instead I told him I'd already purchased a ticket to fly back this upcoming Friday. I hated lying to him but I felt this resolution would be equally gratifying (at least for the moment).

Returning to Hannah's room I discovered that she'd left her id on the nightstand. Below her photo was her birth date. It read November 20, 1969. She was turning 40 in a couple of days. I couldn't believe it. Although I wish it hadn't, this gave me a lot to think about.

Later that day, we rented a few German movies with American subtitles. This was in reward for Emily making a ninety percent on her school exam.

It was the perfect movie setting with popcorn and soft drinks, which created a stimulating family environment. The films we watched would ordinarily peak my interest, but for some reason I couldn't bear any concentration. My mind was boggled and occupied with an orchestra of thoughts that made no sense.

I almost felt as if I were coming down with Scarlett Fever (for this would certainly account for some of the ambiguity I was left with). Frequent and sporadic, my thoughts began charting off in different directions...

The timing of everything happening in my life seemed to be a bit off. The days were short and the nights even shorter. It felt like just the other day I was studying hard for finals in my last semester of college. But in actuality, five years had passed since then. I had come to realize what the older heads really meant by "enjoying life while you're still young". It seems that when you reach a certain period in your life, time begins to increase at an unbelievable paste. I wondered, if this was to remain the case, then how much time would I actually have to enjoy with Hannah? She was turning 40, which left a 13 year age gap between us.

It had only been a week and a half since I'd met her, and already I was contemplating spending the rest of my life with her. Perhaps it was just infatuation, or perhaps she'd cast some sort of spell on me which I was unaware of, but nevertheless I was captivated. When it came down to it, she was the total package.

She was keen on every subject we ever talked about and exhibited my favorite qualities in a woman. She was outgoing and fun, genuine, and not to mention strikingly good-looking. Certainly three times the lady; and come to think of it I was a better person around her. I'd cut back on smoking and swearing. And up until now, my anxiety and stress level was the lowest it's ever been.

Although she never spoke on her feelings towards me, I could most definitely sense them at times. Was I falling in love? I surely was in need of some sort of sign that I was making the right decision by going home. I knew that Hannah would be upset if I told her that I was leaving come Friday. She'd been reminding me of her birthday every day for the past week. Even more, making me promise to come to her party; I felt I had to tell her at some point...

The erratic thoughts roaming about in my head must have somehow altered my appearance; Hannah saw that something was troubling me.

"Mel, are you alright?"

I suddenly came to, as if awakened from a trance state. Holding my hand, she looked

upon me with worry. Again she asked, "Are you alright?"
Still battling with my thoughts, I simply nodded…and finally uttered "just a little tired."
Hannah walked with me up to the bedroom. She then got Emily all ready for bed and shortly returned to my side.

The next morning I was slow to rise. Hannah and Emily had already left for work and school. I truly felt as if I were coming down with something. Whatever it was I didn't want to give it to Hannah or Emily so I searched the medicine cabinet for cold medicine. I couldn't make out what anything was. It was all scribed in German. Not recognizing any familiar words, ultimately I decided to desist.

Nonetheless I still had to do something about the cold that was creeping up on me. To my luck the kitchen offered greater options. I ate a few oranges and prepared some hot tea. I sat down to watch some British news.
The Royal Duchess was being accused of selling access to her ex-husband, the Prince.

I noticed that scandals here in Europe were as common as scandals in the western part of the world. The tea started to make me drowsy. Thereafter, I quickly doze off.

When I awakened I saw that the time was now 1 o'clock and I knew that Emily would soon be getting out of school. I rushed to get dressed, making sure to wrap up with extra layers. Outside, a snow storm was underway.

When I arrived at Emily's school she was already waiting near the shrubs out front, talking with her friends.
On the walk home we passed an old man with a cardboard box filled with puppies. Emily's eyes lit up and she dashed towards them. She began asking the old man a hundred questions, including could she hold one. Right away I figured this to be a big mistake because the next question would be directed towards me on whether or not she could have one to take home.

"Okay Emily let's go now, your mom's on her way to the house to meet us"—I said trying to quickly advert her.

"Oh Mel he is soooo cute. I love him, and look at this one" she picked up another now holding two pups like infants.

The mother of the pups rose to her feet. She then released a low terrible growl that began to escalate.

"Emily I think you should put them back now alright. The momma's getting a little upset. Come, let's go."

The old man walked towards me sounding off prices, trying to get me to buy one.

Before I knew it, I heard Emily belt out a heartbreaking scream.

I pushed the old man aside to get to her. The mother had lunged at her leg and was shaking the cuff of her pants viciously. Without thinking I reached down and grabbed Emily to pull her away but the dog's grasp was still too strong. The old man started yelling at it and prying its mouth open with his hands. I then lifted Emily up as high as I could and suddenly the bottom of her pants leg ripped, at the same time freeing her. When I turned away the dog then proceeded to claw at my leg and repeatedly jumped at my side to get to her. Finally, the old man grabbed a hold on to its collar with both hands.

I carried Emily away to the McDonalds next door to examine her leg. She had stopped crying but was still shaken up leading her to hyperventilate. Luckily there was only a small scratch near her ankle. I tried my best to calm her down as everyone started to look at us. I surely didn't want to give anyone the impression that I was harming her.

A lady that worked behind the counter approached us with a bottle of water. I thanked her and slowly Emily began to catch her breath. I called Hannah at work and told her what happened, and then let her speak with Emily. She told us to stay there until she came with the car because of the snow storm in the midst. In the meantime, I ordered her a happy meal. I figured she wouldn't be hungry with what just happened and all, but maybe if she played with the toy it would take her mind off of it. I glanced outside and noticed snow flurries beginning to fall.

Hannah arrived about 20 minutes later. She rushed in to take a look at Emily. She then picked her up and gave me the keys to the car.

That evening Hannah spent most of her time on the phone. I had no idea what her conversations were about because they contained a mixture of German and Russian. Emily and I watched episodes of Sponge Bob until she fell asleep.

Hannah and I spoke that night, and though it might have been poor timing, I explained my situation to her. When I finished, she then contested that if my leaving was about the dog incident from earlier today that she in no way blamed me for what happened. I assured her it wasn't. Ultimately, she said that she was cool with it and knew that I had to leave at some point.

The whole conversation she never smiled and I could see the anger and frustration in her face and body language. The last thing I wanted to do was cause her more stress.

I started to think about all that she had done for me in the past few weeks. I didn't have too many people back in New York that would have done any of this for me. But what was I to do? If I left I'd feel selfish and consequently if I stayed I'd feel selfish. It was a never ending struggle. That night we didn't make love or even speak much the following morning.

Chapter 13

The night before, I started to pack my things but couldn't finish because of the remorse surrounding me. The weather outside was pretty shitty, which depicted exactly how I felt.
While continuing to pack I came across half a pack of cigarettes in my jacket. Amazingly it had been an entire week since I last had one. I took one from the pack and as I brought it to my lips, something about it just didn't feel the same. Somehow I came to the conclusion that no cigarette could make me feel better about leaving.

The time had come for me to say my goodbyes and although I could see the disappointment in Hannah's eyes, deep down I could see she understood. I pleaded with her to let me take the train to the airport. I couldn't bear to cause her inconvenience on her birthday. Emily grabbed a hold of my leg and cried. I promised to come back and visit her.

"I don't want you to leave", she repeated over and over. A tear came inching near the corner of my eye, but I refused to let it fall. This was to ensure them of how serious I was about coming back to visit again.

"Listen Emily, I will always remember the fun times we had ice skating and singing Christmas songs together. When I come back next year we can do it all over again. Don't worry I'll be back. When you want to talk to me just ask your mom to call me. Study hard and keep your grades up. Okay?"

"Okay."

"Be a good girl and listen to your mom."

"I will."

I looked up at Hannah. The look on her face was a tossup between sad and angry. I gave her a hug and she told me to take good care of myself and to call when I made it home.

As I boarded the train, I couldn't help but feel a wave of grief fall over me. Was I making the right decision?

Shortly I arrived at the airport. Upon entering the terminal I walked towards the flight schedule display. Next to me was a little girl playing with her Sponge Bob toy.

Her father smiled at her as he held her hand; the mother stood next to him interlocking arms. Even with the lines jammed packed and the list of numerous cancelled flights due to the weather, they still seemed so happy to be getting on the airplane together.

Next, the unexpected occurred. The man said to the little girl "*Kommen. Laßt uns gehen Hannah*—Come. Let's go Hannah." The sound of her name resonated in my ear over and over again. It was clear to me that I had unfinished business. I had to go back and let her know how I felt. At once, I left the airport and hopped back on the train headed back in the direction of Haslach.

Chapter 14

When I arrived back at Hannah's house no one was home. I suspected that she'd already left for the party. I left my bags and headed to the club. Indeed, I neglected to call her and decided to surprise her instead.

On the way over, I replayed the scenario over and over in my head. In detail I imagined what I would say, as well as how she would respond. Although the more I said it aloud, the more rehearsed and insincere it sounded. Eventually, I just decided to wing it and speak from the heart.

I arrived at the club in good time. It was half past nine. The club was just as I remembered, but with less crazy shit going on. [But then again, it was still early.] I walked up the stairs into the main hall, and then quickly spotted Hannah's face in the Mezzanine amongst the party decorations.

The closer I walked towards her the more of a euphoric feeling swept over me.

Suddenly, I was stopped in my tracks by an oversized Neanderthal wearing all black. It was the same bouncer I'd recognized from the last time I was here. He had scratches on the side of his dome-sized cranium and a bruise on the left side of his cheek and for some reason he didn't seem happy to see me again. Did he remember me from the fight? Was I about to be thrown out for something that happened weeks ago? Perhaps more importantly, could he have been the one that nearly broke my fist with his face bone? As much as I wanted to, I couldn't blame this one on the alcohol and have all forgiven. I quickly decided to turn and head the opposite way, but I was soon greeted by yet another security figure near the entrance staring coldly at me. Then another on the wall to my left, and by this time they were starting to close in on me.

"Fuck!"

Plainly, I felt like there was nothing I could do, so I began sending an SOS text to Hannah as they came rushing in towards me. Two of them grabbed both of my arms as if to escort me out quickly without causing a scene.

"*Bitte kommen Sie doch mit uns!*—Please come with us!" they said.

They led me to a side door that I hoped would be an exit outside but it wasn't. It was a long and dark dusty corridor filled with storage items. As my heart raced unsteadily, I thought to myself this is it. The end is near. I could see the headlines now, 'A young American man found shot dead in the dumpster of an alley….and he shitted on himself too'.

As we walked closer to the end of the corridor I felt a boost of moral filled with positive but destructive thoughts like going out in a blaze of glory, or at least severely hurting someone. Perhaps, I would find some kind of object to gouge out an eye or a jugular. I had to think fast because we were almost near the end of the hall.

"What's this about? Where are you taking me?"

No answer.

"I'm seriously going to fuck somebody up if you don't let me go!" I shouted. Still no response.

The door opened and in they flung me towards a sofa chair while they stood near the door as if to make sure nobody entered and nobody left. In this room, there was a small office with a desk containing security monitors and a television mounted on the wall. Another man stood near the desk and spoke off in the direction of the wall on a Bluetooth. He was bald and had a small hoop earring. From the gray trimming of his beard, I presumed he was at least fifty or so. He wore a silver shirt with a tailored suit and he was closer to my size, maybe shorter. Naturally, if worst came to worst, I figured he'd be a lot easier to take down. I began planning my assault, browsing the room for things to use as weapons and possible escape routes. No weapons were in plain view but there was a door behind the desk; with my luck it was probably a closet. The tailored suit man, whom I assumed was their boss, started to wrap up his conversation. He then turned his attention to me.

"Hello, how are you?" He asked in a heavy foreign accent.

I quickly stood.

"Please sit!" He said pointing with an open hand.

I took a look at the bouncer, who was now facing me. I sat down.

"Why am I here?" I asked.

"I don't know. Why are you here? Or should I say: why are you back?"

"Huh? What do you mean?"

"Don't fucking play with me! I have you and your friends on the camera destroying my club!" he shouted.

He sat down at the edge of the desk and turned the television on to reveal me and the Italians on tape fighting. Luckily, the person that I'd hit wasn't the bouncer. The quality of the tape was so poor that I could easily dispute these accusations, but then again I was probably the only black person there that night.

"Who is going to pay for this damage? HUH!?" he shouted.

"I mean, how much is the bill?" I asked. [As if I could barter my way out of the situation.]

"Listen to me and listen good. I run a clean business and I don't like American trouble makers coming in and FUCKING IT UP" he yelled followed by some sort of swearing in another language.

All of a sudden, the closet door opened and in walked a short figure wrapped in a throw blanket. I made it out to be none other than Emily. Her eyes grew large and marbled at the sight of me.

"MEL!!!" she yelled as she ran towards me. The man rose to his feet and the bouncers started towards me with fury. I quickly put my hands in the air and stood back.

"Wait! Wait!" The man called them back. He had a very confused look on his face. He then spoke German with Emily. Suddenly, it dawned on me; this was Emily's father, Gino.

They looked nothing alike.

"Are you her tutor?" he asked.

Before I could respond there was a knock at the door. The bouncers braced themselves as they turned to open it.

Suddenly, Hannah walked in, pushing one of them aside as she passed through. I noticed a slight shock in her upon seeing me standing there with my hands up. She walked furiously towards the man in the tailored suit and began shouting at him in German while pointing at me and Emily. She resembled an angry parent that'd just discovered someone having done wrong to her children. "Put your hands down Mel", she instructed me. Her face was completely red and her veins appeared to be popping out from her neck.

I felt very much vindicated by Emily and Hannah's rescue. The man came towards me and apologized in a tone less threatening than before. Aside, he shook my hand and also thanked me for saving Emily from the dog attack a couple of days ago. He then picked Emily up and told me that he was on his way out of the office to take her home when one of his guys spotted me. As I started to apologize for that night, he told me not to worry about anything. In fact, he stated that if there was anything that I needed, to just ask Hannah because it was her club tonight. We bid him and Emily well. Hannah took my hand as we headed back to her party. Just looking at how pretty she looked tonight made me forget about everything that had just happened completely. The moment we got to the other end of the corridor, I stopped to face Hannah. I tried desperately to recall what I wanted to say to her, but I was too distracted by her beauty.

Instinctively, I grasped her in my arms and eagerly kissed her up against the door. At the first pause to catch her breath, she rewarded me with that billion dollar smile of hers.

"Happy Birthday", I whispered.

"I missed you too", she replied.

We rejoined the party where I was introduced to some new friends of hers as well as some I'd remembered from the strip club. Happily, we all danced and partied throughout the rest of the night with champagne overflowing our glasses. As I basked in the moment, this time I made it a point not to black out.

The next day we picked Emily up from her father's place and spent the whole day at the carnival in Bad Canstatt. She had a great time. We all had a great time.

Alas, all that came to an end as Sunday came too soon and it was time for me to set off back to the states to fulfill another promise. Contrary to Friday, it was actually a nice day for flying.

This time I elected to let Hannah drive me to the airport. She even sat and chatted with me until my flight was set to board.

"I have something for you." She handed me a small package.

"What's this?" As I began to unwrap it she told me to open it on the plane.

"It is from me and Emily."

The intercom chimed and stated that my flight was now boarding. Hannah walked with me towards my gate while holding my hand. I stopped and turned to face her one last time. I could see her eyes begin to water as her grin became a full-fledged smile.

"You won't forget me, will you?" she asked softly, with her fingers at the tip of my chin.

"Of course not, and I better see you next year! Or else I'm going to hunt you down" I responded.

She gave me a great big hug, squeezing me tighter than I'd ever been squeezed before. Out of sheer reflex I kissed her lips avidly as if this was really the last time I'd ever see her again. My mind interrupted, signaling me to cease before I reached the point of never being able to let go. As I turned and entered security check point I could feel her watching me as I walked away. I wanted to turn and look back, but didn't in fear of seeing her cry, which would only in turn cause me to cry.

Seated on the airplane, I found myself in a daze staring out the window with a million questions running through my mind. All of which were concerning Hannah and Emily. Questions like: Would she really come to the states? Did she even feel about me the same way I her? Would this be the last time I ever saw her? I even imagined myself storming off of the plane and running back to the terminal hoping she'd still be there waiting at the gate like in the movies. *Surely she'd still be there, right?* The intensity of my thoughts were soon disrupted by the boisterous plane turbines and the fasten safety belt queue.

After takeoff, all of the thoughts continued to cloud my head again. I couldn't bare it any longer so I reached into my bag for the sleeping pills I'd purchased and came across the package from Hannah. I gently opened the wrapping. Inside was a nice leather journal the size of my hand. I opened it to find a picture tucked in the inside of the cover.

The picture was of me, Hannah and Emily that we took at the Schwaben Galerie. The back of it read:

Mel (my beast),

The picture is so you will remember what we look like when we come to visit you in the states lol. The journal is for your writing. Promise me you will not give up on your dreams. You are truly an amazing person.

Love, Hannah and Emily

P.S. I love you :)

I smiled as a tear streamed the length of my cheek. It was then, I finally understood what Andre the bartender meant by abiding by the LLC. Instantly my mind was free of all worries and doubts. I had a strong feeling that everything would be alright. I grasped my pen, opened the journal and began to write.

About the book

Gone to Europe, Leave a Message originally started as a playwright. As the main character began to emerge throughout the different settings, I saw it better fit as a book.

The inspiration for this book comes from that defining time in one's life where change is inevitable. An overwhelming majority of quote on quote "successful" people go through hard times and are left with not so much as a clue with what to do with their lives. Some turn to religion and consulship for guidance, and others tend to seek more unconventional methods (myself included).

The main character depicts a most realistic occurrence. His life is filled with various challenges, as well as self-inflicted doubts in which he must overcome. When he puts his fears aside and decides to take a chance on life, great things happen. I believe this to be a true testament of numerous individuals that have, perhaps, faced similar dilemmas.

Coming Soon:

The District

The Cherry Blossom Effect

The District (preview)

Chapter 1

I once had it all… the mansion, the cars, the women…the entire fucking city…I owned it. And the funny thing is…I always thought there was no possibility of ever losing it, but needless to say there was. So how did this tragic fall from grace occur?

It all began at the Blues Speakeasy Tavern, summer of 1965 in Georgetown. The famous Italian mobster, Benny the Boa Constrictor was in town from New York conducting the usually business. You know, threatening night clubs and hustlers for a percentage of their earnings and expanding his territory. Meanwhile, my father was also there visiting his childhood hero, the legendary jazz musician Dizzy Gillespie.

At the intermission, my old man stepped out into the alley way to smoke a cig. It was then he noticed a few men abusing some helpless broad. Being the statesman and upright citizen that he was, he went to her aid. Tragically, I lost my father that night.

The next morning I was awakened by a shriek that could have wakened the dead. I'd never in my life heard or seen my mother so torn and distraught. I rushed down stairs in my G.I. Joe PJs to discover her wallowing in grief knelt down on the floor as the police stood on the other side of the storm door.

Supposedly, the police got a distress call from the club the night before. Outside of the club, they discovered my father with a knife wound to the stomach. The murder weapon had been found behind a dumpster. Martha Greenwood, a co-worker of my mother, was there that night and had witnessed Benny personally stab my old man with the knife. The news spread like wild fire throughout the district. The case was immediately brought to trial.

After Kennedy's assassination, the federal juries were a lot harsher in cases that involved the killing of government officials; my father just so happened to be on the city council and in the midst of running for council chairman.

In addition to Martha's testimony, the prosecutor had an overwhelming amount of evidence against Benny. All of a sudden, Benny the Boa Constrictor turned Benny the rat. He began snitching on every cop he'd ever paid off. Thanks to Martha's testimony he was found guilty on all counts and sentenced to 28 years in federal prison. My mother was awarded treble damages totaling 1.2 million dollars. How could a black woman receive so much back in those days? That's just it—she wasn't black.

My mother was a white woman from Paris, France. That's where she'd met my father on the way back from his tour of duty in North Vietnam. According to her, when they met is was amour at first sight. My mother never loved any man more than she loved my father.

So now I suppose you're thinking I inherited this great sum of money; not the case. Believe it or not, she actually gave it to me when I turned 16. She no longer wanted it after she discovered that the night my father was killed, he wasn't there alone. He and Martha Greenwood were there together, on a date.

One day while cleaning out my father's liquor cabinet, she opened a cedar cigar box and found a series of love letters, all from Martha. From that moment on she was never the same and nothing mattered to her, not even me. She died a year later from an over dose of sleeping pills.

I was in a catholic school at the time. Being an only child and left with no one to look after me, I practically had to raise myself, but through trial and error so to speak. A young black man equipped with what some might call a fortune, growing up in the 70's era; I did what any rebellious and easily inspired teenager would have done at that time.

For more information on the author and other works visit **BrandonSinclair.com**